Because I Want Him

Just Because, #2

Drew Duncan

BECAUSE I WANT HIM

Copyright © 2021 Drew Duncan
All rights reserved.

EDITING BY: Karen Sanders Editing
FORMATTING BY: Irish Ink Publishing
PROOF READING BY: Proofreading by Mich

Chapter One
Rick

"YOUR HIGHNESS." Bright sunshine streamed into my bedroom, the sound of curtains being pulled ringing in my ears. "You have an appointment in two hours and you need to get up."

From outside the room came the dulcet tones of Hugo Everly, my chamberlain, my 'gentleman-in-waiting' and all-out pain in my fucking arse. "Has that useless reprobate got himself out of bed yet?"

I groaned, rolled over, and pulled a pillow over my head. "No, Sir," the poor groomsman mumbled. I didn't need to look to know he was being ushered out by Hugo. The door slammed shut, and I waited for the barrage of abuse to begin.

"Rick, for the love of God, would you get your pale backside out of bed before I have to drag you out of it."

A grunt was my only reply.

A moment later, the covers were yanked off me where I lay. "Ugh, there's a sight I could have done without seeing this morning."

I chuckled and looked out from under my pillow. "Well,

Hugo, if you hadn't removed my covers, you wouldn't now be looking at the crack of my ass."

"Your *Highness*, you have an appointment this morning. You're heading to the main offices in London of the children's charity you are now the patron of. This is your big press introduction."

I heard the tone in Hugo's voice as he emphasised the 'highness'. I rolled my eyes and sighed. He was right; I needed to get up.

It was the whole reason I was here now, after all. A would-be banishment from my home in Thornbay Palace back in my home country of Solena in Scandinavia. This was meant to be my chance to 'find myself' so I could 'settle down' and be the good little boy Mama and Pa wanted me to be.

My mother was a distant member of the British Royal Family. Not an heir to the throne or anything like that, but it was enough of a connection that I was also afforded a title here, as well as being the heir to the throne of Solena. It also gave me rights to the use of Odiham Castle as the Duke of Hampshire.

But Hugo was right, I needed to make a good impression to counteract my recent 'faux pas' as Mama called it. I had been out on my motorcycle without any of the usual pomp and circumstance, the press had caught on to it, and when I gave them a friendly hand gesture, it was snapped by a pap and went global. Mama wasn't impressed, and Pa was furious. I had suffered a thousand glares from him. 'Not fitting for the King's son to be seen as nothing more than a common rogue.' My parents had put up with a lot from me, I had to admit. I wasn't the usual model of classic monarchy that could be put out on display all the time. For a start, I was one of the first openly gay members of the Royal

Family, and I was certainly the first who was next in line to the throne. I had tattoos, I rode a motorcycle. I was the stereotypical bad boy. I just happened to be a prince too.

"RICK!" came the shout and the matching slap on my bare arse.

I rolled over and glared at Hugo. "You dare lay a hand on the royal person."

He snorted. "You're lucky it was just my hand. Now get the fuck in the shower."

Hugo was my best friend and confidante. We had met at boarding school. I had been shipped off to the best one England had to offer when I was a teen, and of all the things he could have gone on to be afterwards, he joined forces with me as the head of my household, as it were. He was there to look after me, to make sure I did what I was supposed to when I was supposed to. He *mostly* kept me out of trouble, and my mother and father adored him, calling him a good influence on my life. It's the main reason I was allowed to appoint him as my chamberlain instead of some stuck-up insufferable toff. Rich coming from a prince, I know. I groaned and moved my naked frame from the bed and headed into my en suite to flick on the shower and plunge myself under the water.

"What did the family say about the latest round of paparazzi bullshit?" he asked from inside the bathroom.

"Oh, you know, the usual shit. Mama just hmmed and tutted. Pa went off on one about me acting like no more than a commoner and behaving in a manner unbefitting of a member of the monarchy, never mind one next in line to the throne. England was supposed to be making me see sense, not for me to be making a bigger fool out of the family, blah blah..." I sighed, thinking about it. My head was still pounding from the amount of liquid amnesia I had drunk the night before. That morning, I remembered only too well what my mother and father's reaction had been.

He was right. I had come here at my mother's suggestion that I join up with a charity she had done a lot of work for when she was younger. She had connections to it, and it seemed like a good idea at the time.

"Bit harsh," Hugo replied. "I would have thought a mere middle finger was tame by comparison to the last time."

Yeah, thanks for that reminder, Hugo. Last time had been me being caught by the paparazzi, flashing my arse to someone in a nightclub back in Thornbay. The situation was made worse because a rather handsome fashion model just so happened to be slapping said bare arse at that time.

"It's not like I go looking for this shit," I argued.

Hugo's sarcasm rang out in his reply. "Oh, God, no. Heaven forbid anyone would even suggest it."

I opened the door to the shower and stared at Hugo. "Fuck off."

He just grinned at me and kept laying out the fresh towels and my robe, ready for me to get out and get dry. I slammed the door in a huff and went back to attempting to let the warm water soothe me.

"Do you want to hear about this charity?" he asked.

There was no time like the present. I shrugged, silently inviting Hugo to continue

"Right, well, you will now be the patron of a leading children's rights charity. The Domino Trust. You will be doing the usual meet and greet with kids, and you will also be doing the traditional posed handshake for the cameras with the charity's director, Benjamin Roberts."

I leaned in against the marble tile of the shower and hung my head, letting the water pebble down on my neck and shoulders. I needed a massage, but there wasn't enough time for that today, so this would have to do.

"Then what?" I asked through the water running over my face.

"Then it's the usual shit, Rick. Don't say anything that offends anyone, don't do anything that offends anyone, and then get in the car and fuck off home. Now, hurry the chuff up."

This was not going to be a good day.

Hugo ushered me through the rest of my grooming and bundled me into the back of the car, ready to hit the mean streets of London to the main offices of The Domino Trust. "Where is this place, anyway?" I grumbled.

Hugo stared at me. "Just over the Hammersmith Bridge, off Castelnau. Will you get your shit together? We'll be there in about twenty minutes."

He was right. I needed to get my game face on. But honestly, I was still feeling the effects of my hangover and the constant comments I'd been having about my recent behaviour. It was a month ago now, and my father still wasn't prepared to let it go. Hopefully, today would go some way to helping apply a balm to that particular wound.

When the car pulled up outside the charity's main office building, there was already a crowd gathered, ready to wave, snap photos, and generally monitor my every move. The more I did things everyday people get away with on a daily basis, the more of an interest to the media I was. Today was definitely one of those days that would pique their interest. They would be lying in wait for me to make another 'mistake' that would sell them a few tens of thousands more tabloid rags.

"Ready?" Hugo asked.

I nodded, and without thinking about it, I held my breath as I stepped out of the car and into the fray.

All around me were endless calls of my name.

"Prince Frederick! Prince Frederick! If you could just look over here."

Others just asked constantly about 'the incident'.

"Your Highness, do you regret your actions with the press last month?"

I put my best well-practiced warm smile on my face and waved to everyone, saying nothing about giving the press the finger. I made my way along the small line of the standard welcome folks specially selected for the 'honour' and photo opportunity. This was a children's charity, so there were a few kids standing out, waiting for my arrival. There was a pretty little girl in a blue dress with a teddy bear in her hands. I knelt low in front of her to be at her level and offered my hand for her to shake with a friendly hello.

"My name is Frederick. What's your name?" I asked.

She blushed. "I'm Emma."

"Well, Emma, that's a very pretty name for a very pretty girl." I kept a hold of her hand as she talked to me.

She held out the teddy. "This is for you." I took it from her and looked at it. It was a cute little bear, hand-knitted and lovingly stitched.

"He's amazing. Did you make him?"

Again, she blushed. *This kid is adorable.* "I helped my aunt make him."

"Is your aunt here?" I asked.

She shook her head. "No, but that's my daddy over there." She pointed into the building I was due to walk into and I caught a glimpse of the man standing inside who gave her a little wave.

I turned my attention back to the bear. "Does he have a name?"

She nodded. "He's called Bobby Bear."

I looked at the bear in my hands and grinned. "Well, hello there, Bobby Bear. It's very nice to meet you." I looked at Emma again. "I need to say hello to some other people now, but thank you very much for Bobby." I lifted her hand to my mouth and kissed it gently. "It was lovely to meet you, Emma." And then I got up and moved on along the line.

I shook hands, I nodded, I thanked people for coming to see me. Just before I headed into the building, I looked at Emma and gave her a cheeky wink. A smile lit up her face and Hugo ushered me into the building.

"Your Highness, I present to you Mr Benjamin Roberts, director here at The Domino Trust," Hugo announced. "He will be showing you around the building and discussing the work that happens here." He gave me the customary nod and directed my attention to the person he was referring to as the director—the person who had waved to the little girl outside.

"Your Highness, it's lovely to meet you," the man said, smiling with a small bow. I reached out my hand to shake his, and when I took his hand in mine, I looked at him.

Holy shit.

A prickle of electricity ran up my arm and into my body. His smile was so warm and genuine that I couldn't help but respond in kind.

"Very nice to meet you too, Mr Roberts."

"You can call me Ben, if you wish, Your Highness."

I nodded. "Thank you, *Ben*." I smiled.

Damn. Professional visit, Rick. Professional visit. This guy has a kid!

For the next two hours, I walked around the Trust's offices, listening to stories, and listening to staff tell me about their jobs. I asked them about the issues facing the young folks they worked with. I heard the horrible situations some of them were finding themselves in, and I pledged my support to do anything I could to help raise money for them so they could help children more.

"It's funny you should mention that, Your Highness." Ben smiled.

"Oh?" I asked.

He looked a little sheepish; it was adorable on him. "We're planning a big gala dinner for the end of the month, and I was wondering if you would be our guest of honour."

He didn't have to explain further. "On one condition." Ben raised an eyebrow, and I continued. "I'd like you to sit at my table so we can talk about this some more."

Probably not the wisest move I've ever made, and I was probably barking up the wrong tree with this man, but I was compelled to have more time in his company.

Ben grinned and nodded. "I would be honoured, Your Highness."

I could see Hugo looking at me over Ben's shoulder. I knew that look on his face. He could read my thoughts and knew there was something about Ben that was keeping my interest. He gave the tiniest shake of his head. If you didn't know him, you probably wouldn't even have seen it.

Hugo cleared his throat. "Your Highness, I hate to interrupt, but you have another engagement this afternoon, and we have a schedule to keep." He bowed to me. *Asshole.* I knew what he was up to, but I wasn't about to say anything.

I needed to keep up the façade. I nodded in acknowledgement and turned my attention back to Ben.

"It has been lovely to meet you, Ben, and I look forward
to doing anything I can to help this wonderful charity you
have here." I nodded to him and shook his hand again.
Damn, more sparks.

I held his hand in mine for just a second or two longer
than was appropriate and watched as his pupils dilated just
a fraction.

*Well, what do you know? This attraction isn't as one-
sided as it might first appear.*

"Thank you for being here, Your Highness. It's been
lovely to meet you too." He held my gaze, a little more
forward than he should have been. Protocol and all that
bollocks, but I welcomed it, loving the chance to look into
those gorgeous grey eyes just a moment more.

A throat cleared in the background, and I let go of Ben's
hand and broke our gaze. As I glanced at Hugo with the
subtlest of glares, the little girl I had met outside ran up to
Ben and launched herself into his arms. Ben blushed and
grinned at her.

"Daddy, did you see me? Prince Frederick liked my
bear!" Before Ben even had a chance to reply, she turned to
me. "Where is he?" she asked, her little brow furrowed as
she looked at my empty hands. Hugo waved it in her line of
sight. "My friend Mr Everly has him. He was keeping
Bobby company for me while I was busy."

She sighed, her little face still scrunched in an adorable
frown. "Daddy is always busy too." Poor Ben looked like he
needed the ground to swallow him whole.

"Emma!" he scolded. "I'm sorry, Your Highness." His
face was a delightful colour of red. "She's six, and I'm so
sorry." I laughed and held a hand up to dismiss his apology.

"I promise not to take any more of your daddy's time today." I smiled at Emma and put my hand out for her to shake. "Deal?"

She grinned, put her little hand in mine, and shook. "Yes!" She looked at her dad in the 'told you so' way only children can do. I glanced over to where Hugo was still waiting for me, smirking. He and I would be having words later. *Tosser*.

More goodbyes and thank yous were uttered, and eventually, I got back in the car and on my way. I really wanted to find a way to get back to the charity and into the company of Ben Roberts sooner rather than later.

Chapter Two
Ben

Everything around the charity that morning was buzzing. We had never had the privilege of a Royal patron before, and everyone was excited to meet him and see what him being there could do for the charity. While he wouldn't personally be offering money or services, we knew that just having his name with us could do a hell of a lot of good.

I had to admit, I was a little worried. It wasn't as if he didn't have a reputation, but I had been assured that he was aware he needed to improve his public image, and it was hoped his involvement with our charity would be the kind of publicity he needed. I just hoped he would keep his cool long enough to help us see the benefit of it. *Can you 'sack' a Royal patron?* I hoped I wouldn't have to find out.

We were all running around like headless chickens, giving everything a last-minute clean and tidy. Flowers had been put on a few of the desks, and balloons were in the foyer of the building. Everything was prepared, and now we waited.

My daughter had insisted on meeting Prince Frederick. I wasn't even sure how she knew about him, but there was something mentioned about it at school, apparently. She and my sister had made him a teddy bear. I didn't know if that was protocol. I didn't know if it was something that he would like, but my child and my sister are forces to be reckoned with and nothing was going to stop either of them.

The minutes slowed to hours as we awaited the arrival of His Highness Prince Frederick. We had all been briefed on the protocol.

- Men will bow/women will curtsey when greeting the member of the Royal Family.
- You will address the Prince as Your Highness.
- Do not touch the Royal person unless you are touched first, this includes handshakes.
- Do not walk in front of His Highness with your back to him.
- Do not...

The list was almost endless and made me more than a bit nervous on top of the nerves I already had. I had the tour around the building all planned out. I knew where I was taking him. I knew who I wanted him to talk to. I had them all briefed on the dos and don'ts of the situation, and on what to say, for the most part. I wanted him to be impressed. I wanted him to see the charity and be glad he had become its patron. I wanted the charity to have a long relationship with him that made it a lot of money and got it a lot of goodwill. My great-grandmother started the charity herself, and I know she would have loved the direction this had the possibility to take us. I wanted to nurture it for as long as humanly possible.

"Ben! Come quick! The cars are here!" Molly called as she ran to the door. My stomach somersaulted, and my heart started to act like it was trying to escape from my chest. I had never met royalty before, and I certainly hadn't taken them on a tour of my charity before.

Benjamin Orwell Roberts, you have got this, I told myself. I just hoped I was going to believe it.

I put on my best smile, stood outside the door, and waited. The man I knew as the Prince's right-hand man and doer of everything, Hugo Everly, got out of the car first and turned to the back door to open it. He nodded to the Prince that it was okay to exit the vehicle. Molly and I held our breaths.

When he stepped out of the car in a gorgeous, blue, perfectly tailored suit, I heard a very faint 'fuck' puff out of Molly. I glanced in her direction, my eyes wide.

"Sorry, boss. He's bloody gorgeous." She apologised in her most hushed voice. I let out a single laughing breath and smirked. She had a point; he was stunning. Not what you would expect from European monarchy. Strong men, sure. Handsome men, of course. Stunningly beautiful... well, that was something very different, yet there it was, standing before us in all of its six feet of glory.

Mr Everly nodded, and the Prince made his way along the presentation line we had waiting for him. He paused, and he chatted. He was very polite and perfectly approachable. We waited, watching him interact with everyone until he got to Emma. I held my breath and watched, hoping she would remember to be on her best behaviour. To my surprise, the Prince was amazing with her. Slowly, he made his way over to where we were standing.

Mr Everly paused in front of me, facing the Prince and waiting for his attention. "Your Highness, I present to you Mr Benjamin Roberts, director here at The Domino Trust." He gestured towards me. "He will be showing you around the building and discussing the work that happens here." He nodded, and I knew it was my turn to speak.

"Your Highness, it's lovely to meet you," I said with a smile and a small bow. To my surprise, Prince Frederick offered his hand out to shake mine. I gratefully accepted, shaking his hand firmly. A sudden warmth spread out over my body from the point his skin met mine. *Damn*. I smiled warmly and was greeted with the same in return.

"Very nice to meet you too, Mr Roberts."

My mouth opened, and the words fell out before I had the time to think too much about them. "You can call me Ben, if you wish, Your Highness." I know my face flushed a little when I said it. I was being far too informal with him already.

Fortunately, he nodded and agreed. "Thank you, *Ben*." If I wasn't mistaken, there was a particular inflection in the way he said my name.

You're probably imagining things.

I gestured to my right and introduced him to Molly. Her official title didn't do her justice. She was my right-hand woman, and she was as instrumental to the charity as I was.

"Your Highness, I would like to introduce you to Molly Harrington. She's the assistant director here at the charity, and I would be utterly lost without her."

The Prince smiled, Molly curtsied, and we started our tour of the building. "Lovely to meet you, Ms Harrington. Will you be joining us on the tour?" he asked.

Molly grinned and gave me a little bit of a side-eye. "I would love to, Your Highness, but while Ben is showing you around, I have a meeting with our legal team about our new venture."

Oh, clever girl, Molly. I smirked when I heard her comment. She was very casually dropping our biggest project to date into the conversation before she headed upstairs to finalise the ownership and conversion of a building we had been gifted in a donation made in the will of one of our charity's dearest friends and supporters.

My plan had been to walk him around the building and let the heads of each department tell him about what they did. But the longer I was in his company, the easier I found it to talk to him. On the first floor, I introduced our social working staff. Their head of department, Miriam Dodds, chatted to him. He seemed genuinely interested in the work the team did.

"And would you go out to the children living rough in London regularly?" he asked me as we headed up the stairs to the next floor.

"Well," I explained, "a lot of these kids really believe they are better off on the streets than they would be having our support properly. Which I can understand. They've mostly come from backgrounds where people have let them down time and time again, and the sad truth is, they just don't trust us. So, we have a van that we can load up with food, drinks, and basic hygiene products, and we head out most nights. It means we see most of the kids we know on a two to three-week basis. And until they trust us, we will keep doing that kind of thing for them. We're just trying to prove to them that not everyone is going to let them down, hurt them, or use them. Of course, we worry about them the most, because they're at risk of so much living on the streets. Trafficking, sex working, drugs, and of course, assault and sexual assault. Many of these kids have started out with the odds already so stacked against them, and they end up here with no one to turn to."

Prince Frederick nodded, listening intently. "Do you get many homeless children who do eventually trust you?

What I mean is, is the programme of going out to visit them on a regular basis working for them and you?"

I stopped before I opened the door to the main second-floor space and considered his question. "Well, I think without a doubt it's working for them. We're showing them that some people still care, and that can never be a bad thing. As for it working for us, even if it only lets us get one child off the streets, and it's achieving more than that already, then I would say it's definitely working for us as a charity. Saving even one child from the hell that is living rough is my life's work." I grinned at him, pulled open the door, and gestured for him to enter.

We spent the next two hours touring the building, talking to the teams, and explaining all of the things we have achieved and would like to add in the future. I told him all about our new half-way house, the very building Molly was talking to the legal team about, and I asked him if he would be willing to attend our gala dinner. I was hoping his presence would generate more ticket sales and that it would also lend up more publicity about the new project itself.

When we finally made it back down to the front door, Prince Frederick turned back to face me and offered his hand to me to shake again. "It has been lovely to meet you, Ben, and I look forward to doing anything I can to help this wonderful charity you have here."

I didn't doubt him for a second. He was warm and genuine, and he showed a real interest in supporting the charity and its work. He held my hand in his for a little longer than he should have. I felt that same warmth creeping over my body where his hand touched mine. In any other circumstances, with any other man, I might have asked for his number, but that was obviously not even a consideration here.

Instead, I grinned at him and my gaze lingered for longer than protocol probably allowed. "Thank you for being here, Your Highness. It's been lovely to meet you too." I held his gaze, definitely being a little more forward than was allowed with the next in line to the throne, but the longer he held on to my hand, the more emboldened I felt.

A throat cleared in the background and the Prince let go of my hand and glanced at Mr Everly. It was at this point that Emma was true to her authentic self. She came barrelling past the Prince, leaping at me and leaving me no choice but to grab her.

I could feel the heat creeping into my cheeks. I knew that, strictly, he was here to make a good impression with us, but I wanted him to have a good impression of me and the charity too.

"Daddy, did you see me? Prince Frederick liked my bear!" I didn't even have a second to reply to my little imp before she looked the Prince up and down and didn't find what she was looking for. "Where is he?" she asked, pouting with a crinkled brow, staring at his hands.

The Prince's assistant jiggled her gifted bear in his hands.

"My friend Mr Everly has it. He was keeping Bobby company for me while I was busy." She sighed. I didn't know what she was going to say next, but I knew it was going to show me up in a way only Emma ever could. "Daddy is always busy too."

Oh, Jesus!

"Emma!" I tried to scold her, knowing it wouldn't do much good. "I'm sorry, Your Highness," I blurted out, embarrassed. "She's six, and I'm so sorry."

His face lit up in a laugh, and he held his hand up, silently telling me my explanation wasn't needed.

His handsome features suddenly got very serious. "I promise not to take any more of your daddy's time today." He smiled, putting his hand out for Emma to shake. "Deal?"

She chuckled, put her modest, unusually clean hand in his, and shook it as hard as she could. "Yes!" Her look said it all. She had out manoeuvred me, again. I shook my head in defeat.

There were a few more nods; 'thank you' and 'look forward to working with you' was uttered. Then he turned on his heel and was ushered back to his car by his staff. A few seconds later, he was gone.

Molly patted my back and stuck her tongue out at Emma. "It's all good, boss. I think that went pretty damn well!" I cast a silent prayer to the heavens that she was right, cuddled my little girl tightly, and tried not to think about how much I wanted to see the Prince again.

Chapter Three
Rick

I GLARED AT HUGO. "I don't know what the hell you think you're talking about."

"Rick, you were practically drooling."

"Oh, fuck off. I wasn't."

Hugo laughed at me and started to mimic what can only be described as the voice of a teenage girl. "Oh, *Ben*, it's been *so* lovely to see you. I can't wait to work with you more." Then he stuck his fingers in his mouth like he was trying to be sick.

"You have to be the biggest cock I've ever met."

"Only because you can't meet yourself."

"Peasant."

"Snob."

Both of us laughed. "You did like him, though, right?"

I winced. Part of me wasn't sure if I wanted to admit that to myself, never mind someone else. "I don't know." I shrugged. Liking someone was a luxury that wasn't afforded to someone like me. There was no dating in the same way others could. There wasn't the freedom to just go out to the clubs with my friends. I wouldn't be able to take moonlit strolls hand in hand with my boyfriend along the Thames. There was nothing normal about dating when you were a member of the Royal Family.

Hugo gave me *that* look. "I know. I get it, and he has a kid. Didn't see that one coming. But, for what it's worth, I'm still pretty sure he bats for your team. And you know, people in your family do meet people, date. Hell, they've even been known to get married."

I glared. "Do not, ever, mention the M-word around me!"

Hugo threw his hands up with a laugh. "Right, okay. Prince Frederick will never have a husband, or children, or anything else, and the whole monarchy will die with you."

I stared at him in disbelief. Was that really what was going to happen? Did I really have to get married and have a child to keep the family going? Couldn't I just leave that to my younger brother, Alex? I mean, he was the respectable one of the two of us. He was the one already married with a pretty young wife who was already bearing his heir. If I adopted a child, would they have the same rights to the throne as a bloodline heir? I'd probably have to get the backing of parliament or something for that, or worse still, the agreement of my father. *Why the fuck am I even thinking about this?*

He laughed even more. "Dear God, I just watched you try to figure out if that was something you would actually do. You must like him if you went as far as thinking about that!"

"Oh, fuck off, or I'll have you shipped off back to the dungeons of Thornbay for treason and let the tourists poke you through the bars of your cell."

"*Rick and Ben sitting in a tree, k-i-s-s-i-n-g.*"

He kept laughing, and I was about to get up and punch

him in the balls when someone knocked on the door of my private apartment. "Enter," I growled.

One of the staff entered with a note for me on a tray. He bowed and presented it to Hugo. He lifted it, read it over, and nodded. "Please tell the Lord Chamberlain that Prince Frederick will be available presently." The footman bowed again, turned, and left.

I looked over at Hugo with an exaggerated eye roll. "What now?"

"Facetime with the folks. Probably just looking for you to go over what happened today with them." He shrugged.

I sighed. "I don't know why they can't just ask the Lord Chamberlain to ask you. That's what he's there for, after all."

Hugo grinned. "And miss out on the chance to personally kick you in the nuts over your behaviour again? Pa couldn't possibly!"

He was right. I had to be honest, it was starting to get old. I appreciated that I had behaved 'in a manner unbecoming to a member of the Royal Family,' but I hadn't done anything racist, and I hadn't done anything dangerous. I had given a hand gesture to a bunch of members of the press who would have thought nothing of hounding me and chasing me all over Thornbay just to get a damn photo to sell to the highest paying gutter tabloid.

Thousands of people give someone else the finger on the roads of Solena every single day. I do it, and the entire world loses their mind, including my parents, King Albert and Queen Helena. I resigned myself to the fact that I would now have to go and see them, explain how the day went, and tell them just how thoroughly committed to working with The Domino Trust I really was. At least I wouldn't have to lie about that.

I sat in front of my laptop, waiting for the connection with my parents. Hugo sat beside me and let out a chuckle. There were times I wished I could just have been tarred and feathered and got it over with.

"Your Majesty, Your Royal Highness, His Royal Highness Prince Frederick is now connected to you as requested."

I heard my parents thanking the Lord Chamberlain, and they pulled their laptop in front of them. I nodded to acknowledge them.

"Mama, Pa, you wished to see me?" I smiled politely. I was getting as skilled in this particular protocol as I was at the polite smiles and thank yous when I met the public.

"Freddie, my boy. How did everything go today? Tell us what happened."

No-one had called me Freddie since I was a child. I shook my head. "Thank you, Pa. I was invited to a gala dinner event for the charity in just a few weeks."

My mother smiled. "I'm glad you got on so favourably there, Frederick. It is a lovely charity, and they do some magnificent work for children. I knew it would suit you when I suggested it."

She was right in one respect. Spending more time with Ben Roberts was going to suit me a whole hell of a lot. I smiled at her and blew her a kiss. "You have always been wise, Mama." A quick look at Hugo and I saw his subtle eyebrow raise. Yes, I was indeed flattering my mother to get her on my side. She was the only one who was able to get through that thick skull of my father's.

"I hope you understand now, Freddie. We can't have any more scandals. You're making a mockery of the monarchy, and I won't stand for it."

"Now, Bert," my mother scolded. Hugo gave an almost

imperceptible eye roll. I flashed a slight smirk. That was all it was going to take. I didn't need to say anything else because my mother would now put my father firmly in his place. I listened to her start to lecture him on not lecturing me, and Hugo watched in amusement.

"Pa, Mama, if you will excuse me. Today was very successful, and we need to plan how best to support the charity now, Hugo and I. Forgive me." I bowed to my parents and nodded to Hugo who promptly ended the video call.

"It never ceases to amuse me how easily you can get your mother to challenge your father on your behalf."

I snickered. "It's a gift."

Hugo eyed me carefully. "So, you need to plan more contact with the lovely Ben, do you?"

"You know as well as I do, old boy, there's a lot of protocol involved when you have a member of the Royal Family to a dinner event." I was pushing my luck, I knew it, but I needed to have Hugo on board with my plan to see more of Ben. He was my greatest ally in the world, and he was also my lifelong best friend. It was why he and I worked so well together.

"Old boy? Christ, you're such a toff," Hugo scolded, and I just grinned.

Chapter Four
Ben

Jesus Christ. I wasn't even into the house with Emma when my sister had the front door open and was asking me questions.

Emma grinned and ran to her aunt, hugging her at the hips. "He was lovely, and he likes daddy, and he loved Bobby!"

Ashleigh looked up at me and raised her eyebrow. "He likes daddy, huh?"

I shook my head. No, that was *not* what was happening. I walked up to my two favourite ladies and kissed my sister on the cheek. "Not like that." I glared, lifting my eyebrow to silently tell her not to push it.

She smirked at me, and I knew she wasn't going to drop it. The second Emma was tucked up in bed, the next game of twenty questions would begin.

"Hungry?" she asked, looking down at Emma, whose little face lit up as she nodded. I had to admit, the smells coming from the kitchen were amazing and beckoned to my now empty stomach.

Ashleigh handed me a glass of wine and sat on the sofa opposite. "Well?"

"Well, what?" I asked, pretending I had no clue how this conversation was going to go.

She glared. "The Prince."

I took a sip and thought of how I wanted to reply.

He was gorgeous? Yes, he was. But that wasn't the opener this conversation needed.

He wasn't as bad as the press made out? Also true, but no, that also wasn't where I wanted to go.

He was the easiest man in the world to talk to? Yeah, no. Not going there with my kid sister.

In the end, I settled for, "He was really good with Emma. She seemed to be quite taken by him. He was very gracious about the teddy."

Ashleigh looked at me like I had a second head.

"Really? *That* is where you're going to go with this conversation?"

I closed my eyes and took a longer drink from my glass, readying myself for the next part of the conversation.

"What do you want me to say, Ash?"

"He's gorgeous."

"He is."

"He is very obviously gay."

I gave her a 'no shit' side glance.

"So?" she pressed.

I laughed at her. "So? So, he's gay, and I'm gay, and that must mean we need to jump each other?"

She sighed. "You're a dick," she said and took a drink from her own glass.

I knew once I admitted I liked him Ashleigh would

never let me hear the end of it. But I also knew if I said nothing, I would overthink it to oblivion, and by telling Ashleigh, I would purge that from my mind and be able to just get on with it.

I closed my eyes and let my head rest on the back of the sofa. "I liked him. He was easy as hell to talk to, and in another universe, I *maybe* would have offered him my number. As it stands, just as we were saying goodbye and I thought there might have been a connection, Emma ran over, jumped at me, and I'm sure I saw a look from him when she called me daddy. So, whatever it was or wasn't... it isn't."

I opened my eyes to find her grinning at me.

"You like him!"

I sighed. Right then, I remembered why I shouldn't say a word to my little sister. Sometimes, my overthinking of the non-existent situation was one hundred times better than the look she was giving me right then. That shit-eating, she knows something I don't and I'm about to never hear the end of it, grin.

I drained the last of the wine from my glass, handed it to her, and told her I needed a re-fill. Hell, with what I knew she was about to launch into, I was going to need the whole bottle.

Chapter Five
Rick

TWO WEEKS LATER, I was sitting in Ben Roberts' office, discussing the finer points of the dinner event he would be having in a week's time. This wasn't a publicly announced visit, so there was a lot less pomp and circumstance around it. Instead, we were on sofas overlooking the city in the corner office at the top of the charity's building, drinking coffee, and talking about how he found himself as the director of a charity at such a young age.

"It was my great-grandmother's charity. She set it up to protect the children who were working and sometimes dying in the mills back in the day. There were no laws to protect them back then. The mill owners rarely paid anything when a child was killed or injured in their employ, so she set up the trust to make sure, at the very least, that they didn't end up in the workhouse because of what happened. She was a bit of a revolutionist, my gran."

I grinned. I couldn't help myself. The warmth with which he spoke of his family member radiated from him. She had apparently been a formidable woman. She probably would have had a lot in common with my own mother. "She sounds like she was a genuinely remarkable woman."

Ben grinned, clearly remembering something about his great-grandmother that touched him. "Oh, she really was. I have some fond memories of her. She was one of seven with several older sisters, and she used to tell me she would sneak into her older sister Mary's wardrobe and borrow her brand-new dress to wear to the dance with my great-grandfather before Mary even had the chance to wear it. She joked about how much she'd got away with it, and how she'd always managed to sneak it back into the wardrobe without Mary knowing. I remember her sister telling me years later that she knew fine rightly the dress had been borrowed, but that their mother wouldn't have approved of them bickering with each other, so she just let it go and pretended she didn't know."

I nodded and appreciated the story until Ben turned to me, and I could see the change in his expression as the colour rose in his face. "I apologise, Your Highness. It was rude of me to prattle on like that about my gran."

I waved a hand in his direction to dismiss his comment. "Not at all. I'm enjoying hearing about her, and I have to be honest, it's nice to be talked to like a human being instead of some stuffy protocol-needing robot."

Ben's eyebrows furrowed.

Jesus, had I really just denigrated the traditions of my family and my station to him? I inwardly groaned and slowly blinked while a short puff of breath expelled from my lungs as I attempted to remember who I was and why I was there. "I fear it is now I who must apologise for prattling on. I'm not used to behaving myself, as the press likes to remind me."

He graced me with a grin. "Oh, I've seen some of the

things you've had printed about you, Your Highness. I'm sure it's mostly a *bum* rap."

Did he just make a pun about my arse? Is he flirting with me? He held my gaze again for just a second longer than he should have.

"Dear God, you saw that article?" I laughed. "Well, then I definitely need to apologise to you for having the audacity to get my pale derriere on the front cover of almost every national tabloid we have."

He grinned more and blushed a little. He was looking at me with a hint of something. I could tell he was thinking of that image that had been on pretty much every news outlet there was all over the world. It had taken at least six months for the veins in my father's forehead to not stick out when the incident was mentioned. It was three years ago now.

"And now I have reminded you of my arse, and again, I apologise sincerely." His face flushed just a little redder. I grinned smugly. Talking to Ben was the most natural thing in the world, and he made the whole thing so effortless. "Relax, Ben," I said, touching his arm. "We stopped locking people in the Tower for what they might be thinking years ago."

He snorted with laughter and touched my hand as it rested briefly on his arm.

Fuck. This man is far too easy to be myself with. It's going to get me in trouble.

There was a knock on his office door, and Hugo appeared around it. I let my hand drop from Ben's arm, knowing only too well that it was too little too late, and my best friend would be harassing me about my breach of protocol. Again. I did feel sorry for him. He was charged with keeping me out of trouble, and instead, just like it was when we were kids, I was able to end up leading him into the thick of it. Bless him; he did have an unusual ability to interrupt things just as I was getting a little too forgetful of my duties. A handy skill, even if it was a little frustrating from time to time.

"Ah, Your Highness, you have another appointment to attend today. We have to be back in the car in approximately forty minutes." He nodded to Ben, and to me, and closed the door behind him.

"Your best friend?" Ben asked.

"Since we were kids in boarding school." I smiled, admitting more than I should have.

"Sorry, Your Highness. I shouldn't pry. It really is none of my business."

I waved my hand in dismissal. "Actually, as long as you keep it between us, I don't mind telling you. You're very easy to talk to."

"I was just thinking the same about you."

Again, he held my gaze, and something hung in the air between us. I needed to change the subject. I needed to stop looking at him quite so closely. "Is there a Mrs Roberts?" I asked him, hoping he would say yes and I could talk myself down from that ledge.

"Only my mother." He smiled.

I nodded. "Just never met the right woman?"

He snorted again. "More the right man. I'm gay, Your Highness."

Shit.

"I know what you're thinking. But I have a daughter, right?"

I shook my head. I wanted to hear that story, but I wasn't sure it was ever going to be my place to ask.

"She's mine via a surrogate. Time was marching on, and with everything else I have in my life, I wasn't sure if I was ever going to meet 'the one' and settle down and have a baby, so I arranged a surrogate. I was young to choose that path, but it felt right to me then."

"Oh, you're still young," I dismissed.

"I'm thirty-eight in January. I think my mother has given up hope of ever getting more grandchildren or having to buy herself a hat."

I looked at him, confused. There was no way the man in front of me was four years older than me. He looked like he was still in his late twenties. "I'm sorry, what? You can't possibly be almost thirty-eight!" I scoffed. "You look younger than me and I'm thirty-four!"

The blush was back on his handsome face. "Thank you, Your Highness. You flatter me."

"There's not a hint of flattery in it, Ben. I promise you."

"You're very kind."

I winced with a smirk. "Let's say honest rather than kind; it's much more believable." Again, he laughed, and the sound echoed out in the office, wrapping itself around me, feeling like the most soothing sound I'd had the pleasure of hearing.

We kept chatting for the rest of the time I was there. I had to admit, there were a few times in the course of the morning that the comfort and ease Ben instilled in me had me almost insisting a few times that he called me Rick. I couldn't quite make myself say the words, though. I didn't want to push my luck, and I didn't want to open myself up to that particular can of worms with Hugo and my family.

Instead, I left it as 'Your Highness' and thanked him honestly for spending time with me, discussing his family's legacy. I told him my staff would be in touch about the finer details of the dinner and that I would see him in two weeks when he would be a guest at my table.

Chapter Six
Rick

In the time leading up to the dinner event, I didn't have time to see anything more of Ben. Hugo had that pleasure, and he assured me Ben and his staff had been fully briefed as to what was and was not allowed. The event was a sell-out, and the charity was already feeling the benefit of having a member of the Royal Family as a patron. Personally, I thought they might have fared better with a celebrity endorsing them, but I wasn't going to turn down any chances to be around Ben now, and even without Hugo's friendly banter, I was very much aware that made me sound like a love-sick teen girl.

My attentions were required elsewhere. Pa had asked me to go to Australia on his behalf. He had an invitation from the Prime Minister, Les Wilson, and he had another engagement at a similar time in Canada.

"Car's here," Hugo announced, dragging me back to reality.

I nodded. "You sure you can't be persuaded to come with me?" I laughed. Hugo shook his head. He had no interest in visiting Australia. The Prime Minister had a worse press than I did. I'm pretty sure that was why Pa was sending me in his place. Next to that guy, I would look like a fucking saint. "Didn't think so," I said, grabbing my coat. "Wish me luck." I smiled.

Hugo smirked. "Just don't punch the fucker, no matter what he says and how deliciously tempting it might be. Think of the press."

I rolled my eyes in reply. This would be *fun*.

Just over twenty-four hours later, I was sitting on the tarmac in Canberra Airport. "We're sorry about the hold-up, Your Highness." Claire, our flight attendant, smiled apologetically.

I frowned. "What's the delay, do you know?"

She looked out the window and grimaced. "Prime Minister Wilson hasn't arrived to meet you yet."

I sighed and rubbed my head. *Brilliant*. The fun and games were starting already, and I hadn't even got off the plane yet.

"I assume we haven't heard anything yet as to why, just that he's not here?"

Claire shook her head. "Sorry, Your Highness. Nothing has been reported as yet."

"Thanks, Claire. Any chance of a coffee while we wait?" She smiled, nodded, and headed for the galley.

I exhaled and tried to relax, settling back into my chair, and grabbed my tablet. I could at least reply to some emails and have a look at some news, and maybe even play a game or two in the time I was going to have to wait for Les Wilson to bother getting his sorry arse to the airport.

An hour and a half later, without any reasons or apologies, the Prime Minister finally arrived, and I was able to get off the damn plane. I got to the bottom of the steps, and there was Les, grin on his face, hand outstretched to greet me. When I took his hand, he pulled me in against him with his other arm around my shoulder and smiled for the cameras like he was greeting a business client for a photo opportunity. Inwardly, I was already disgusted by his behaviour. Outwardly, my best well-practiced smile was firmly in place.

"It's lovely to have you here in Canberra, Your Majesty. Welcome to Australia."

I saw the look on my aide's face. I even saw the look on Les's wife's face. Only a king or queen is the bearer of the title 'Majesty'. I hadn't even been in his country for two hours yet, and already he was acting like a complete moron. His wife looked like she was about ready to let the tarmac swallow her up, and my aide looked like she was about to break off his arm and remind him of his place. *That I would pay to see!* This was going to be a long fucking trip.

When I finally made it out of the airport, I spent another twenty minutes heading over to Government House. I just wanted to get into a bed. I was exhausted. It had been a long flight, and I wasn't the best of sleepers when I was on a plane. Les had other plans. As soon as I walked in through the door, he was commenting on the itinerary again.

"So, Your Majesty, I thought it would be a good idea for you to talk to some of the charities we have here in Canberra. I know you've started supporting some charities yourself. I also thought it would be nice if we could have a dinner on Thursday evening with all the usual stuffy folks."

I just wanted to get out of there. I nodded. "Excellent,

thanks." I didn't wait to hear his reply. I followed my aide and disappeared into my quarters while I was on my visit.

"Your Highness, I am so sorry about the breaches in protocol you've been experiencing already."

I smiled at Jennifer, the aide. "Think nothing of it. Believe me, I know only too well this isn't something you and your staff have messed up. A bit like myself, the Prime Minister has a reputation that precedes him, I'm afraid." I hoped she would appreciate that I understood who was at fault in the situation.

She laughed nervously. "Thank you, Your Highness. Is there anything I can get you before I leave you for some rest, Sir?"

I shook my head. "No, thank you. Sleep is all I need for now."

She smiled and headed back out of the room, leaving me to get under the covers to catch up with so much of the sleep I had missed out on in the last twenty-six hours.

When I woke, I had a few texts and missed calls from Hugo. Apparently, the news of Les's lateness had made its way back to Solena and the UK and was all over the tabloids, as usual.

> *Saw you had been stood up on arrival. Nice to see he's still as charming as ever :/ This is why I didn't go with you!*

> *Try not to kill him before you leave – think of the publicity ;)*

Text me when you wake up, you lazy twat. Got any
messages for the lovely Benjamin? haha

He really was such a knob sometimes. I needed to have words with him, again, when I got back to England. I hit reply.

You're an arsehole. Pretty sure if I did him in,
our Royal Guards could make it look like an
accident. Might even be doing the Australian
public a favour ;) Also, yes, tell him all the
protocol and dos and don'ts that you're meant to
be telling him and nothing else, you fuckwit.
Love you x hahaha

It was time for a shower, and to see what the hell was planned for the rest of the day.

"Hi, Jennifer," I said as I walked into the main study of the apartment I was staying in.

"Good evening, Your Highness." She smiled. "Can I get you anything, Sir?"

I shook my head. "I assume there is something planned for this evening?"

She nodded. "Prime Minister Wilson is holding a cocktail reception in your honour. It's here in the grounds, so it would be easy to retire from if you so wished, Your Highness."

I grinned. "Thank you, Jennifer. Hopefully, it might not come to that, but this is Les's party, and the night is still young, so one never knows what might happen!"

She snorted. "Yes, Sir. Would you like a light supper brought up to you before you get ready?"

My stomach growled in agreement with her suggestion,

and I laughed. "I think that might be a good idea. Thank you."

She nodded, got up, and left to get me something to eat. In her absence, I took the chance to gather my thoughts on what was happening with this trip so far. I hoped that while I had been asleep, dear old Les had been re-briefed on the finer points of dealing with royalty. I knew that made me seem like a snob, but where the Australian Prime Minister was concerned, I was glad there were such strict rules I could enforce on him. He was an idiot.

I walked through the reception, led by the Prime Minister, nodding, smiling, and shaking hands. Each person was greeted with a cringe-worthy comment.

"Your Majesty, this is Bob Linus. He's the head of an LBTG charity here. I'm sure you and he would have a lot to talk about," he announced. Bob openly winced, and the PM headed off for a moment in the other direction.

"I'm so sorry, Your Highness." He laughed nervously. "I'm an LGBTQ charity director here. The Prime Minister tries to be an ally."

"Bob, that's very polite of you. I think your Prime Minister needs to try some more. It was lovely to meet you, and I hope to be able to talk to you a little later about your charity." Just as I finished speaking, Les Wilson reappeared at my right-hand side.

"There are a few more people I would like to introduce you to, Your Majesty, if you would just come this way." Again, he put his hand on my back and directed me towards a group of people standing nearby.

Several hours later, I was standing again with Bob

Linus. "So, you help teenagers with issues of coming out?" I asked.

Bob nodded. "Yes. It can be hard. Not every family is approving. Not every family is accepting. I'm sure Your Highness can appreciate that it's not always an easy thing to tell people, and when their reaction is less than favourable, it can be so destructive for these kids."

I agreed. "Despite my background and how supportive my family is, there was nothing as terrifying as coming out to them, and then afterwards coming out to the entire nation and world, hoping they would accept me just as I am. The title doesn't negate from the same trials and tribulations of that particular circumstance."

He smiled and bowed his head in agreement. "I hadn't thought of it in those terms, Sir."

I laughed and touched his arm for a second. "Don't get me wrong, it's nothing as harrowing as these young adults and teens are dealing with, but I can completely understand what their circumstances might leave them with. It's a terrifying process, even when the odds are in your favour." I smiled. "I would love to do anything I can while I'm here. I've just become the patron of a children's rights charity back in the UK that has a worldwide reach. The Domino Trust. Have you heard of it?"

"I have, Your Highness. They are very well thought of, and what we have here is a very similar venture specifically for LGBTQ youth. Anything you would be willing to do here would be very much appreciated."

I thought about it for a second. "You have a drop-in centre, don't you?" Bob confirmed they did. "Why don't I call in there and just have a look around. I'll bring the press and get you some coverage. Would that help?" I held out my hand again for Bob to shake.

"Your Highness, that would be incredibly generous of you. I know you've got a very busy schedule." He smiled, shaking my hand again.

"Not at all, Bob. Not at all." I smiled and made my apologies to leave the group. Jennifer was standing on the sidelines, waiting. I approached her, explained my conversation with Bob, and asked her to arrange the meeting I had agreed to and to make sure that the international press was at the ready to attend the drop-in centre with me. I also asked her to make my excuses for the evening. I was weary after an evening in the company of Les Wilson, and I needed more sleep.

Chapter Seven
Rick

Other than the general annoyances from a Prime Minister that just couldn't get the rules of behaviour into his thick skull, the next few days went reasonably well. That morning, I was heading to the charity I had been talking to Bob Linus about. Prime Minister Wilson had decided it was in his best interests to make the most of the press opportunity and tag along to the charity with me. A fact I was less than impressed about.

I strode over to Bob when I got out of the car and extended my hand for him to shake with a smile. "Mr Linus, lovely to meet you again." I was mindful of the journalists beside us and stood smiling, letting the paparazzi have their chance to get the photo they needed. Then I let Bob walk us into the drop-in centre.

He happily showed me around the facility. I talked to staff, I talked to kids, and I listened to everything I was being told as a few select members of the press followed us around. Les was surprisingly quiet the whole time.

"I think what you're achieving here is magnificent," I admitted. "It's lovely to see these young people being given a second chance to have somewhere safe to be with people who accept them just as they are." I was honest. This was a place I was sure Ben would love to have seen for the Trust back in the UK.

"What happens if a *normal* kid needs somewhere? Would you turn them away?" And there it was. Les Wilson's intelligence shining through.

Bob could see what was coming just as clearly as I could. He thought about how to best say what he needed to. "Well, we're specifically here for those who are homosexual or bisexual, queer, and transgender."

I nodded.

"You don't think that's just a little exclusionary?"

I smiled. "Prime Minister Wilson, I think you're missing the point a little bit here. This is a charity specifically for members of the LGBTQ community, in the same way Women's Aid is specifically for women. It's to represent a section of our modern society that may otherwise not have the loudest voice." I really hoped that would be enough of an explanation for him. I watched the cogs in his mind turning, and I watched as the journalists who had been allowed access to the meeting were practically salivating at how this was all playing out before them.

"I don't think that's very inclusionary. Why should one group have something specific to them? It should be for everyone."

One of the paps snorted. If I could have face palmed, I would have. Bob didn't know where to look, and yet again it was left to me again to talk Les down from this particular ledge.

"Well, Prime Minister, I think sectional organisations like this one are a valued part of our society. We are so diverse these days that organisations can't possibly hope to be skilled enough to deal with all the potential issues that may arise without some sort of specialisation to one specific group of individuals, be it on the grounds of gender, religion, race, or sexual orientation. That's why Mr Linus's wonderful charity exists. To do all of the amazing work they do."

Bob smiled. "Thank you, Your Highness."

"You're welcome," I replied warmly.

And then it happened. Les Wilson's mouth opened, and both his feet went in, in the most imaginative way possible. It wasn't something anyone could have predicted.

"Oh, come on now, Your Majesty. He's probably only got you here because he thinks you're a PILF and thinks this will help."

There was a moment just before everyone truly realised what Mr Wilson had said when I thought about whether I would get away with swearing and laughing in his face. Then I thought about my own charity at home, and I knew I had to do anything I could to protect that reputation.

"Uh, Prime Minister Wilson, did you just call His Highness a 'PILF'? As in, like, a 'MILF', only a prince?" one of the journalists asked for clarification.

"Oh, you heard me," he replied.

"And you're aware what that actually means?"

"Of course I bloody do. Someone you'd like to have sex with."

I glanced at Bob, who looked like he wanted the ground to open and swallow him. The surrounding journalists were looking from me to the Prime Minister like it was a tennis match, waiting for my response. They were waiting to see if I would give my typical rebellious attitude to the situation.

I decided to give it the best diplomatic effort I could. I turned my back on the Prime Minister and directed all my attention to Bob. "Mr Linus, I would like to thank you for your time and your efforts with your wonderful charity, regardless of the attitudes of certain members of society and the poor light they shine on it. I believe that behaviour is so more much illustrative of their own prejudices and ignorance than of any wrongdoing on your or your charity's side. It has been a delight to see all the superb work here today, and if there is anything I can do to further help your charity, please let me or any of my staff know, and I will make sure it is done." I smiled politely and shook his hand.

The Prime Minister stood there looking clueless.

"Ladies and Gentlemen," I said turning to the press, "I would like to thank you all for coming at such short notice. I and the charity appreciate your support." I smiled sweetly, gave a side glance to Les, and walked off in a different direction with Bob Linus, leaving the Prime Minister to his own devices.

Bravo mate, I would have punched him for that fucking comment. It's all over the press here. They've been comparing him to other idiot politicians with their moronic comments. Such a fucking knob jockey.

I chuckled to myself when I read Hugo's text about the events of that morning. It had gone global in a matter of minutes. The press here was reporting it all the time. They had public opinions being given on the comments, on the general attitude to the Prime Minister, and if they thought he was worthy of leading the country still. It had imploded. Jennifer had come in an hour or so later to tell me that Bob Linus had been on the phone to apologise, and to also thank me for coming. After it went viral on all the news outlets, he had already had several calls, pledging his charity hundreds of thousands of dollars in assistance.

I sighed in relief, sank back on the sofa, and replied to Hugo.

What about Mama and Pa?

His reply came back fast.

Singing your praises for a change. The old man thinks you really couldn't have handled the situation better. Result, lad. Well done.

I grinned. A charity had more support in an hour than it would have had otherwise, an idiot had made a complete fool of himself and lost the respect of his whole country, and my parents were happy about my involvement in a news story for a change. I had to admit, this hadn't been that bad of a trip to Australia after all.

Chapter Eight
Ben

I HAD BEEN VERY impressed with how His Highness had handled the situation with the Australian Prime Minister. I had several calls from new supporters, offering assistance and finance in any way they could. I was working on the final arrangements for that evening's dinner event when my phone buzzed.

Hello, Hugo Everly here, just checking that every-thing is sorted as it should be for this evening, and that you will be at the same table as His Highness?

I replied that I would be at his table, that everything was sorted, and everyone had been told what was expected of them. I couldn't wait. I was looking forward to seeing more of the Prince and maybe getting to talk to him a little more. It was getting late in the afternoon, and I was letting everyone away early to go and get ready for the evening. If I wanted to get myself well-groomed, I needed to head home too.

A few hours later, I was sitting in the opulent event

space of Grand Connaught Rooms in the heart of London. The room was amazing, from the ornate vaulted ceiling to the chandeliers hanging from it. I made my way to the table of eight where I would be sitting with the Prince, and I waited. I had Molly with me at the table for moral support in talking about the charity. After announcing that the Prince would be in attendance, we had sold every ticket, and I couldn't wait to tell him how well it had gone, and to say thank you.

I stood as he approached, as protocol dictated. He had to sit first. The whole table smiled and nodded, and he took his seat beside mine. "Good evening, Ben." He smiled warmly.

"Good evening, Your Highness. How was your trip to Australia?" I beamed back.

He winked. "Oh, I think you might have seen exactly what happened while I was there. It made every news outlet all over the world, I believe."

I chuckled. "Yes, I did see Prime Minister Wilson was putting his foot well and truly in it again."

He leaned in a little closer. "That's one way of putting it. The man is an asshole, between you and me."

I laughed at his candour. "I would agree with that, Your Highness. He is, unfortunately, well known for it."

He nodded and took a sip from his wine glass. "Agreed."

"You handled him very well, though." I grinned, thinking of how he had left the PM with egg on his face. "I think the press seemed to enjoy your handling of it too."

He chuckled. "Makes a nice change for them to report me in a good light instead of the usual fodder I seem to feed them."

"I hear there's talk of him resigning."

He nodded. "I think he hit about as low as he could with his comments. He went from laughingstock to liability, and I don't think the Australian public wants to tolerate him any longer."

I took a drink from my glass and listened. I agreed with his estimations of Les Wilson. I didn't think there would be much more of his behaviour that would be tolerated. His resignation was expected within the next day or so. The country and his political party were done with him.

Soon, the first course arrived, and the chatter at the table was a little more general. We went from Prince Frederick's trip to the most interesting trip everyone at the table had been on. He led the conversation, engaging everyone. I had to try to prevent myself from looking a little cow-eyed at him.

"I'm very impressed with how full the event is," he commented as his main course was set in front of him.

I nodded. "Well, that's mostly down to you, Your Highness. We had an influx of ticket sales when we announced that you would be attending, and we had another influx when your dealings with Prime Minister Wilson went viral. Between that and the financial contributions that came in, we have enough now to completely finish the new half-way house."

"I meant to ask you about the half-way house. Was this a property the charity had to purchase?"

"The building was gifted to us by a benefactor, a property developer called Aiden Monroe. He's a dear friend of the charity, and thanks to the contributions your patronage has helped us gain, we are financially capable of finishing it already. Well, once we have the painting and decorating done, that sort of thing. We use volunteers for that so it doesn't eat into our budget and we can spread the funding further."

He took a drink from his wine and looked at me. "Is there anything I could help with there?"

I chuckled. "Not unless you're any good with a paintbrush, Your Highness. Honestly, it's good. We have a lot of people willing to get their hands dirty and help." If I wasn't mistaken, his face fell a little with my comment. "Besides, you've already helped so much. We wouldn't be able to even complete the project so soon if it wasn't for your support."

He sighed with a bow of his head. "Okay, well, if you need anything at all, all you need to do is ask. I'm always willing to help, even with a paintbrush."

"Thank you, Your Highness. That's very sweet of you."

"Oh, I'm not all that sweet, Ben. I just might as well help any way I can."

There was an undertone in what he said, and it made my skin prickle. I wanted to tell him I thought he was very sweet, and that, despite everything, he was quite an honourable man, but it was never going to be my place to pay him such a personal compliment, and that was a damn shame. Before I had the chance to overthink it and talk myself out of it, I reached into my jacket pocket and pulled out my business card with my mobile number on it. I offered it to the Prince. "If you really want to help out, call me or text me, and I'm sure we could sort something out."

He looked at me with a grin. "Thank you. Is this your personal number?"

I nodded. "It is. Feel free to use it. Anytime."

His eyes sparkled with something, and he had the sexiest smirk on his handsome face. He tucked the card into his pocket while he held my gaze. The look was interrupted by a dessert being served to the table. The rest of the evening was passed with general chitchat and polite conversation.

I hoped Prince Frederick would find some reason to text me or call me. I didn't really care why.

Chapter Nine
Ben

Ashleigh was still awake when I got home. I didn't really expect anything less.

"How was your date?" She grinned as I plonked my arse down on the sofa beside her.

"It wasn't a fucking date."

"What would you call it then when you're sat at the same table as the man you fancy for a glam dinner?"

I shook my head in exasperation. "At a table with six other people. With a mountain of protocol to be obeyed, because, you know, it's not like he's just some average guy, he's a bloody prince, Ash. That comes with some expectations."

"So, he's wealthy and he has connections."

My sister really was incorrigible. I knew she was well-meaning, and I knew she was being a smartass to wind me up. But the evening in the Prince's company had been truly lovely, and she was kind of marring that a little.

She read my face well. "Am I killing your buzz?"

"Just a bit."

"He nice to talk to, then?" she asked.

I tried to bite it back, but a smirk crossed my features before I could stop it. "He *really* is. And not in some stuck-up way. There's just something about him."

"I still think you're going to end up loved up."

I sighed, but before I could raise my complaint, she continued.

"I know you, my brother. You're a lovely man, and there's no reason he would be able to resist you, prince or otherwise. *You* are just as easy to talk to and just as easy on the eye."

And there it was, the reason—despite the bullshit teasing—I told my kid sister more than I should have. Because she was my biggest fan and would always have my back.

I patted her knee and smiled. "I gave him my number."

She just grinned at me and said nothing. I took her silence as the blessing it was and asked how Emma had behaved.

"Oh, you know. We ate cookie dough, bounced on your bed, and once she was done being sick, I put her to bed with a little whiskey."

I sighed.

"Come on, Ben. Good as gold as always. She's a lovely child as well you know."

Ashleigh was right. I had been very lucky with the little girl who had stolen my heart six years ago. But as Ashleigh would remind me, Emma was the sum of her parts. Her surrogate had been a good friend of mine, and I was her biological father. She was a product of two delightful people, as my sister frequently put it. That, and I was fortunate enough to have the help of Ash when looking after her.

"I'm going to head to bed," she announced, and I

welcomed the idea of being alone with my thoughts about the Prince.

"Sleep tight, kid." I grinned.

"Hope he uses your number." She smiled back, patting my shoulder, then she rounded the sofa and headed for the door.

Me too, I thought. *Me too.*

Chapter Ten
Rick

I COULDN'T WAIT to use Ben's number. I sat staring at the card he had given me that night when I got home. I thought about it for a while, trying to think of any reason to send him a text. It was about three days later when I finally figured out an excuse. I was out on my motorcycle, and I had stopped down a country lane in Surrey when I texted him.

Hi Ben, this is Prince Frederick. I'm in the area. Would you mind if I called in and talked to you about the half-way house?

I held my breath and hit send.
I waited.
Minutes later, a reply came in.

Hello, Your Highness. I'm free in an hour if you want to call by my office?

I grinned and replied.

See you there!

I would need to get a move on if I wanted to be at the charity offices on time. I started my bike up and headed back down the country lanes.

Ben smiled and sat back. He was always so animated when he was talking about the charity. He had just spent the better part of an hour telling me everything he wanted to achieve with the new half-way house. Helping people really was in his blood.

"Can I help?" I asked again.

Ben shook his head with a bashful smile. "It's just painting and all the usual mundane stuff. Nothing exciting."

"Sounds perfect," I interrupted before he said the words I didn't want to hear. Some reason why I couldn't *possibly* be interested because I was in the Royal Family, and, you know, we didn't do tasks like that.

"You want to paint and sweep and help out with general maintenance." He looked at me with a smile.

"Why the fuck not?" I smiled back. "Sounds like just what I could do with. A touch of the 'normal' instead of protocol and pompousness."

Ben nodded in shock. "Okay. If you're sure, Your Highness."

That did it. I couldn't take it anymore. "Ben, may I ask something of you?"

Ben nodded.

"In future, when we're not in the usual 'official' meetings, can you call me Rick? I can't help but feel like 'Your

Highness' is a bit of a barrier. Obviously, when protocol dictates, you will still need to call me that, but when we're chatting like this, or I'm helping you out, can you just please call me by the name my friends and family use?"

Ben stared at me like I had just asked him to cut off my arm.

I smiled at him. "I know it's hard to believe, but I'm just a *relatively* normal man. Same thoughts, needs, wants as you, I just happen to have been born into a family that makes it all a bit interesting."

He nodded. "I'm sorry. I know I've probably been a bit insensitive in that. I would be happy to call you by your name, Rick, when the moment allows for it."

I grinned when I heard him say my name. It made me smile more than it should have, but I wanted him to feel more comfortable around me. I wanted to not constantly be reminded of why my attraction to him wasn't so smart in the circumstances, with all of the etiquette and practice that would be stacked against it.

"How about we start again?"

Ben's brow creased, and I held out my hand to him.

"Hello. It's lovely to meet you. I'm Rick. What's your name?"

His smile spread wide across his face, and he put his hand in mine. "Hi, Rick. It's a pleasure. I'm Ben."

I felt the same pull when his palm touched mine. There was definitely something between us. We paused there, waiting, neither of us wanting to break that connection, shaking hands for no reason other than the contact. His eyes moved to my chest. "Is that a tattoo?"

I had forgotten it was there. I let go of his hand, opened the top of my shirt wider, and looked down at it. "Yeah. That's my dragon."

Ben stepped closer and peered down under my shirt to the dragon tattoo sprawled over the left-hand side of my chest. The scent of his body wash and cologne drifted across the small space between us and flooded my senses. I looked up at him, unable to take my eyes away.

"I'm not usually a fan of tattoos, but that is magnificent," he breathed, then looked up. I held my breath. I wanted to lean forward and close the gap between us. I wanted to press my lips against his, but no matter how much I wanted it, I couldn't will my body to move. In that split second, I waited, hoping he would do what I couldn't. Ben clearly had more sanity than me, and more sense. He sucked in a little breath, cleared his throat, and took a step away from me.

Bless you, Ben. You're a stronger man than I am.

"If you really want to help, we start tomorrow, over at the new half-way house you visited two weeks ago. Eight a.m. sharp. And wear something you won't mind getting messy."

I nodded. "I will see you there in the morning. Thank you."

He smiled at me, and I knew I needed to go because I got pulled into those eyes again and looked for more. I turned on my heel and headed out of the office to where Hugo was waiting for me.

Hugo grinned when he saw me. "You told him to call you Rick, didn't you?"

I laughed and shook my head. "What, have you got spy cameras on me or something?" I patted down my person like I was looking for a bug he had planted.

"No. It's more that you look more relaxed than you have coming out of that office in a while, so either you got a little something while you were in there, which isn't even *your* style, or you got rid of the whole awkward Royal Family stuff."

I shrugged. I knew it made me seem like I was ungrateful for my rank, and for all of the amazing things being born into the Royal Family offered me. But sometimes, it was too much. It was so overpowering that it felt like it could crush me. It was duty, and it was rules, and it was demanding. It was, in some circumstances, lonely, and all I wanted to be was a human being with the ability to love, date, swear, and all the normal things other people took for granted.

Hugo noticed my silence and read it correctly, just like always. "I get it, Rick. I've seen first-hand how it makes you feel. As long as he knows when he still needs to call you by your official title, I can't see it ever being an issue."

"Thanks, mate. I appreciate it. I really do." He patted me on the back, and we headed outside to the waiting cars.

Chapter Eleven
Rick

I WALKED into the half-way house in jeans, a t-shirt, some trainers, and a baseball cap. I kept my head down and waited until I saw Ben, and then waved with a grin. He walked over to me with a smile. "You look different."

I shrugged.

"It's good. You definitely look ready for a hard day's work."

He was right. I was. I needed something to ground me that wasn't me out on my motorbike, pissing off the press. Again.

"If you're any good with a paintbrush, do you want to join me up in the attic space? We're going to have it as a social area, pool room, that kind of thing." He sounded enthusiastic about the possibilities for the space, and it was catching. I willingly agreed to help him, and we and two others headed up the several flights of stairs into the area we'd be working on.

We set to work, covering the floor with dust sheets and masking off all the windows and everywhere else that didn't need paint on it. "There's going to be a different colour on each wall, guys, so since there's four of us, I figured we could do a wall each. Rick, if you want to grab that tub there and do that wall with the windows." He pointed at a pot of sky blue paint and the left of the room. A few people looked my way, some with confused expressions, but I think the fact that I hadn't shaved that morning, and that Ben was calling me Rick, was enough to convince them that whatever idea they had of who I was was wrong. "Lydia, if you want to grab the pinky colour and do the wall opposite to Rick's. Alan, you take that nice light green and do the far end up there, and I'll have this pale yellow and do that wall ahead of me." We all listened, picked up our paints and paintbrushes, and got to work.

I could feel Ben's eyes on me within about twenty minutes of starting. I was carefully making my way around all the edges, cutting the colour in against the lines where the walls and ceiling and base boards met. "What?" I laughed. "Have I got paint on my face already?"

He shook his head with a smirk. "I was just wondering if you had much call for painting in your other job because you're a damn natural."

I glared with a grin. "Oh, funny. I'll have you know that when Mum wants to paint the living room, I'm her man."

Ben raised an eyebrow, knowing full well I was talking shit. But the two other people in the room just laughed and kept painting, and I relaxed into hoping my identity was mostly secret.

The hours ticked by, and the room was really starting to take shape. One of the other volunteers arrived around noon with cups of coffee for us all, and sandwiches, crisps, and some fruit. We all sat around on the floor, having a chat and what was, essentially, a picnic.

"So, what about you, Rick? What do you do in your day job?" Ben watched the conversation carefully. I could see him tensing, waiting for my secret to be out.

"I'm in public relations." I smiled.

Alan was studying me. "You know, you look a lot like Prince Frederick," he stated matter-of-factly.

Lydia replied before I had the chance to with a snort. "Have you got paint on your glasses, Alan? He looks nothing like Prince Frederick. He's not hot enough. No offence, Rick."

Ben choked on his coffee, and I just laughed out loud. "You're not the first person to mention it, Alan. I did actually offer my services to one of those celebrity double agencies, and they happened to agree with Lydia. They didn't think I looked enough like him."

Ben was staring. I knew he was trying to decide if I was joking about that or not. Unfortunately, I wasn't. I had honestly gone to a look-a-like agency and offered my services back when I was about eighteen; it was a dare from Hugo. I went in, they said I looked nothing like me, and turned me down. It was the source of a lot of amusement around boarding school in our final year. I nodded my head to confirm that was true. He laughed softly and shook his head.

I smiled. I liked that I could read him and he could read me too. There's a lot to be said about the power of non-verbal communication when you're in the public eye. Alan eyed me suspiciously some more, and Lydia suggested we got back to work. Thank God. I didn't like being the centre of Alan's attention. I was enjoying being myself, as much as I could be. I was also enjoying the opportunity to be around Ben without any of the usual protocol in the way.

We kept working. Lydia and Alan finished before us, and they headed off to other areas to see what help was needed.

"Typical. They're finished, and we're stuck with the fiddliest parts of the room that take the longest," Ben grumbled with a smile.

"You know what this room really needs, don't you?" I asked, absently staring at the wall. Ben waited for the rest of my comment in silence. When I realised he hadn't replied, I looked over at him. "Oh." I laughed. "Sorry! I was daydreaming a little. It needs a mural of some sort. Something graffiti-looking in style. Urban. Edgy."

Ben studied the wall I was looking at and cast his eyes around the room. "You might be right. It's looking very much like a child's nursery at the minute." I followed his gaze. His point was valid; it was in pretty pastels and looked more like a room for a young child, never mind a social room for runaway street kids.

"Any good at graffiti?" He laughed.

"Funny you should mention that." I grinned, and he stared. I couldn't help it, I burst out laughing. "No, graffiti is not one of my talents. I'm artistic at heart, but I've never dabbled in street art."

Ben laughed too. "For a second there, I thought you were going to tell me that was something else you had tried your hand at. You never cease to amaze me."

He had stopped painting and was standing, looking at me.

"There's a lot you don't know about me." I grinned at him.

"Oh, I don't doubt it for a second."

"I could give it a go in the art terms in here if you wanted. Maybe something in the style of Banksy?"

Ben nodded. "Really? It wouldn't shock me if *you* were Banksy after all the surprises you've been throwing at me today!"

I grinned, and Ben eyed me suspiciously.

"I could get the kids to come up with something themselves. Let them be part of their own space." He had decided I wasn't going to out myself as the legendary graffiti artist after all. And I had to admit, he had a fair point. They might be more inclined to get behind keeping the place nice if they were part of the force that had decorated it.

"Might be wise to ask them to see what they want to put on the walls first, though. You don't want to end up with nothing but cartoon cocks or something."

Ben snorted. "Thanks for that mental image, Rick. Yes, I will indeed vet what they want to put on the walls. This isn't my first rodeo."

I laughed. "Yeah, that was a little patronising of me. Sorry. Anyway, I'm done with the blue if you want a hand with the yellow."

Ben agreed. He still had a bit to do because, every time he was getting somewhere, someone came to ask him to decide something, or to come and check on something, so he was a little further behind than the rest of us. I lifted a paintbrush and got started. As I did, again, someone came to ask Ben a question. As he was talking to them, he was distracted from what he was doing, and his paintbrush collided with my arm. I looked at him in mock shock, my mouth hanging open. He stuck his tongue out at me and kept talking to the person who needed his help. I dipped my paintbrush into the pot, and heavy with paint, dabbed it against his cheek.

The girl he was talking to chuckled, and I went back to painting like nothing had ever happened. "Thanks, Ben." She grinned. "I'll let you get back to work now." And she left, giggling to herself.

"Really?" Ben asked when she was gone. "My face? I only got your arm."

"You should wear that colour more often. It looks good on you." I laughed. Ben dipped his paintbrush and wiped it down my face in a revenge attack.

I turned to him, knowing I looked like I was really pissed off.

"Oh, shit!" His hand instinctively covered his mouth as he tried to hide his laugh. "I'm sorry!" He chuckled. I wiped my hand over my face, and then wiped my hand over his.

"You, Mr Roberts, are an ass, and you've asked for it now," I said, painting a line down his arm.

Ben lifted his arm and wiped it down my t-shirt. "Ugh, it's cold!"

I gasped. "You did *not* just wipe paint down my t-shirt!"

He laughed. "I might have."

"Treason!" I announced, rolling the 'r' more than I needed to.

Ben gasped. "Well, then it's a good job I didn't do this!" He painted directly down the front of my t-shirt. "You might have ordered my beheading!"

"I may still!" I joked. I pulled my t-shirt away from my body to survey the damage. "This was my favourite t-shirt."

Ben looked a little sheepish. "Shit. Sorry."

I laughed. "I mean, it was a few quid in a supermarket. Hugo got it for me especially for painting, but..." I let my voice trail off, dropped the t-shirt, and looked at Ben.

His fist connected with my arm. "You're a shit." He laughed, and I just grinned at him.

"Yes. Yes. I am. But I'm growing on you, and I'm very helpful for a future monarch, you have to admit." I laughed.

Ben blushed. *Christ, he's sexy when he does that.*

"Maybe." He smirked and went back to painting the wall.

Chapter Twelve
Ben

I was pleasantly surprised by Prince Frederick. He was making an effort with both the press to improve his reputation, and with the charity. I was very happy to acknowledge I was wrong to have concerns about him coming on board with us at the Trust.

My phone chirped, and I grabbed it to see who needed me next.

Hi, Ben. Just thought I would see if there was anything else you need help with. I enjoyed myself decorating the half-way house last week. Got any other jobs for me?

It was from the Prince. I grinned when I saw his name and his message appear on my screen. I swiped to open my phone and replied.

Hello, Your Highness! There's nothing to be done with the half-way house as yet, but there is something else you can help with if you'd like?

I hit send and was surprised to get a reply almost immediately.

What else would you like to have me do?

I blushed reading his response. *That's a loaded question.* There were definitely a few things that came to mind that I would have him do, but none of them things I would ever discuss with a member of the Royal Family. It was a shame too. The man was incredible, and there was definitely something between us, but he was a prince, and I was a 'commoner', and a single dad. I knew enough about the history of the monarchy, even a European one, to know that the likelihood of anything happening between us was slim to none. I couldn't help but feel a bit disappointed. I shook my head to snap myself out of my wallowing and daydreaming, and I hit reply.

> *I was going to go out on the streets of London, if you think security would allow it for you, and check on some groups of homeless kids we know about. We usually take them a self-care pack, toiletries, a few snacks etc. If you want to help, I'd be happy to have you along.*

Again, his reply was almost instant.

When and where? I'll be there.

I bit my lip, wishing the undertone I was imagining was actually there. It would be something I would enjoy, being able to text him and have him come and see me whenever I wanted. I wished that was something I could have. *Damn, what is wrong with me?* I was in the middle of a ridiculous unrequited crush, like a love-sick teenager. I needed to get a grip of myself. This was a prince, for Christ's sake, and our relationship was purely business. He was using the charity to improve his tarnished reputation. That thought made me wince. I didn't like to think so badly of him. He wasn't 'using' the charity. It wasn't like we weren't getting anything out of the situation. I hit reply again.

Meet me here at the main office at eight p.m. tomorrow night? We have a vehicle in our underground car park here. If you need to use the car park yourself, the code is 3471.

I didn't need to wait for his reply.

Consider it a date! Look forward to seeing you again.

I stared at his last message for about five minutes, trying to convince myself I needed to let go of this crush, trying to explain to my heart that it didn't need to flutter because he didn't mean it like that. Finally, I closed my phone and set it back on my desk so I could get on with my work. I was being ridiculous, and I needed to get my emotions in check before tomorrow night. Of course, thinking about seeing him wasn't exactly making me calmer, so I got back to work in a vain attempt to distract myself.

Chapter Thirteen
Rick

I WALKED OVER TO BEN, and for a second, he didn't recognise me. "My beard isn't that bad, is it?" I asked with a chuckle.

"Rick? Wow, I almost didn't know it was you!"

I stroked my facial hair. "Do you like it?" I asked, genuinely interested in his opinion.

He thought about it for a moment, taking the time to really look at me. I almost felt like I was being eye fucked, and I kind of liked it. "It's very sexy." He smirked.

Damn. Yeah, that'll do for me.

"Sorry. I probably shouldn't be so forward." He blushed.

I shook my head. "Hell, no. That's all good with me. You can compliment me as often as you like. We're already kinda breaking the rules. You do call me Rick."

He went a little redder.

"Feels good being a little naughty, doesn't it?" I teased and waggled my eyebrows. I really couldn't help myself when it came to Ben.

He gave me a sexy little half glare and raised an eyebrow in my direction.

"So, what are we doing this evening?" I asked, to distract both of us from the tension that was building between us again.

Ben waved keys in my direction. "Are you any good at driving a Transit van?"

I shrugged. "I drove something similar when I was in the military." It was something that was required of all royal males. We all did some sort of service in the military. Pa had been in the Solenian Air Force. I had been in the army, in the 1st Mechanised Corp. Armoured vehicles were a little bit bigger than this van, so I figured I would manage.

"Catch." Ben smiled and threw the keys at me. "Let's go," he said and headed for the passenger side of the van. I went to the driver's side, got myself settled, and started out into the streets of London at night.

"Where to first, boss?" I asked as we drove over the bridge and into Hammersmith.

Ben looked down at the information he had in front of him. "Head for the London City Airport and we can narrow it down once we get there?" I agreed and drove out the way I had been asked.

"So, how's the half-way house going?" I asked, making small talk as we drove across London.

"It's coming along really well. I have to sort furniture soon. Are you any good with a flatpack?" he asked with a smirk.

I glanced over at him. "I'm sure I could manage. I mean, they all come with instructions, right?" I grinned.

He snorted. "They do, but I'll bet you can turn your hand to anything if you really want to."

Oh, I'm sure I could. I can think of something I would love to turn my hand to.

"I can certainly try if you'd care to hold my hammer for me."

He shifted on his chair and stared out the side window into the London winter evening. I really should have stopped teasing him; it wasn't fair of me. For whatever reason, Ben was still a little wary of giving back as good as he got. Perhaps that wasn't such a bad thing. One of us needed to have control over whatever was slowly simmering between us.

"So, what are we doing this evening?" I needed to change the subject, and I hoped that would be enough to bring him back into the conversation.

I felt him relax beside me, and he turned back in my direction. "Well, you know how I explained there are kids who don't trust us enough to come in yet?"

I nodded.

"Well, we like to keep an eye on the most vulnerable, and we head around the city where we know them to be, looking out for them, making sure they're safe, and that they have anything they might need, and just trying to prove to them that we will be here for them no matter what."

"Makes sense," I agreed, keeping my eyes on the road. "And does it work?"

"It does. Don't get me wrong, there are kids I have no doubt will never come to us. But I know that, even though they won't, we're trying to do something to not just abandon them like their families and circumstances have."

I was impressed with his devotion to the children his charity was set up to support. He had the biggest heart and a real passion for what he was doing. "You're very dedi-cated, especially considering it's not really in your job description. I mean, you have a kid of your own at home too." I smiled.

He was silent for a moment, and when I glanced over, he was lost in thought. "I didn't just walk into the position of director because of the family connections I have to the charity, you know. Well, I did, but it wasn't just that."

I glanced over and met his gaze as we were stopped at a red light. "How did you come to it, then?" I wanted to know. I wanted to find out more about this man. I didn't think I would ever get enough. I wanted to know him intimately, in more ways than one.

"I have a degree in social work. I didn't want to just run the charity to make a difference. I wanted to get my hands dirty and properly make a difference to these kids. I went to the University of Edinburgh where I got my Bachelor's in Social Work, and then I went on and completed a Master's too. I volunteered with a local homeless charity while I was in uni, and then I went to Manchester, and I worked with Centrepoint. Three years ago, my father wanted to retire, and I was called on to take over."

Goosebumps rose on my skin. "You're amazing," I said tenderly. "I mean, you really are just an amazing, giving, caring person. You're willing to go above and beyond to help these kids."

He was blushing scarlet red when I looked at him.

"You're quite like that yourself too, you know that, right?"

I laughed. "It's nothing like what you've achieved. I'm a spoilt brat born into a life of privilege."

He nudged my arm. "You are a generous and caring man who was dealt a hand of rules and restrictions, Rick. Yet you still go out of your way to try and do more than protocol allows you to. You ignore the rules and use it to help make things better. I mean, you're here now, driving a Transit van, no security in sight, just so you can be out here helping."

Now it was my turn to blush. I felt the warmth creeping up my neck and over my face. "I'm a mostly selfish man, Ben. I will always have some self-serving reason for doing something."

I could see him wondering about that statement out of the corner of my eye. I thought about whether or not I would be honest with him and tell him what my selfish motive here was if he asked. I wasn't sure, and I never got to find out because Ben didn't ask.

Conversation instead shifted to the wonderful little girl I had met that first day. How he came to have her, who was looking after her when he was working so hard. I laughed when he talked about his younger sister. She sounded like she would be a lot of fun, especially if she too could make her brother blush in the way I was starting to find so damn sexy.

When we got into the area around London City Airport, Ben directed me to places I wasn't even aware existed. We pulled into an alley and Ben jumped out of the van. He grabbed a bag from the back and headed towards some kids huddled in a corner behind some bins, tucked in against a doorway.

I watched the kids smile as he approached and greeted them. They were happy to chat with him and take everything he was offering. He was even offered a hug here and there. I sat in silence, watching him work. It was clear these kids trusted him, even if they didn't admit it or allow him to help them further. There was a relationship there, and he was nurturing it and looking out for them.

After five minutes or so, he jogged back over to the van

and jumped in. "Right, reverse out of here and head back down that road again," he instructed. I saluted with a grin and started up the van to do as I was told.

A few hours went past, and the temperature was really starting to drop. Ben was barely getting warm in the van before he was out into the winter weather again. "Why don't I do the next few and you can stay in the van and get warm this time?"

He looked at me like he wasn't sure that was a good idea.

"It's fine, honestly. I promise."

"Okay." He shivered.

I smiled, grabbed his bag, and headed out into the cold in his place. I walked over to the kids he had pointed out.

"Hi. I'm here with Ben. Are you guys okay?"

They eyed me suspiciously, looking back over at the van. Ben waved to them out of the window.

"You a new guy?" one of the young lads asked me.

"I am. Do I look that obvious?" I smiled.

"Ha, yeah, bruv. You look like a lamb in a pack of wolves."

I laughed. He wasn't wrong. I had done many things in my life, some of them dangerous, and some of them stupid, but this made me nervous as hell. I wanted to make a good impression. I wanted to do Ben proud.

"Well, you wolves better be nice to this lamb. Is there anything you need?" I asked.

"Aside from not having a dad who isn't a punk-ass bitch who beats on me, you mean?"

Ouch. "Well…" I didn't know what to say; I was floundering. Shit.

"Tee, why you always gotta be a dick, innit? Leave the bloke alone and stop giving him a hard time," the girl who had been previously quiet commented.

"Tsk…" Tee sucked in air between his teeth and walked off.

She kept her eyes on him and watched him strutting away. I could feel Ben's eyes on my back. "Ignore him. He don't trust no-one. He ran away because his dad hit him, yeah, but I think it hurts him because he knows his mum was left in that situation."

This kid was awesome. I nodded. "You're very smart."

She grinned. "Thank you, Your Highness. I know I am."

My eyes widened and so did her smile.

"It's all good with me. I can keep a secret." She winked. "I'm Donna, by the way."

"Donna, you're a legend. Do you need a supply pack?" I was grateful for her honesty, and I was grateful for her taking pity on me.

"Yeah, and can I have one for Tee? I know he needs one."

"You can." I smiled and offered my hand to her. She shook it and smiled. "It was lovely to meet you, Donna. Take care, and I might see you again sometime."

She smiled and winked, and I turned to walk back to the van and get in.

"How did it go?" Ben asked when I got in beside him. "Did Tee give you shit?"

I snorted. "You knew he would, didn't you?"

Ben grinned. "Maybe."

I shook my head. "Yes, he did, but Donna came to my rescue." I didn't tell him she had recognised me. She was a nice girl, and something about her told me she wouldn't tell anyone anyway.

"She's a good kid. She's only seventeen and she's been out here for four years. She looks out for Tee. He's the only reason she's still out here. She trusts us and probably would have let us help her over eighteen months ago had it not been for Tee. He's not ready, and she won't leave him out here alone."

"That's really sweet of her. Are they together, or related?"

Ben smiled. "He's sweet on her, but she won't do anything without being in a proper home in case she gets pregnant."

"She's even smarter than I realised." I smiled.

"She's bloody awesome. She loves Tee, and she is very loyal, but keeps her wits about her and keeps us informed of what's happening."

I started the van. "So, where to now?"

"If you head on down this street, I'll direct you over to the next stop on my list."

I smiled and drove off in the direction I was told to.

Chapter Fourteen
Ben

I watched him as we drove around London. It was a chance for me to admire him while his focus was on the road. His long scruffy, early beard looked damn sexy on him. I enjoyed drinking him in while the opportunity was there. While I knew I wouldn't be able to do anything more with him, despite what his flirting would suggest, I could enjoy the window shopping.

"I've warmed up if you want me to take over going out again," I told him, rubbing my hands together. I wasn't completely warm, but I was aware that he might be noticed, and I didn't want to risk his safety any more than he already was.

Rick shook his head and glanced in my direction. "Nope. You're still cold."

"Honestly, I'm okay," I lied.

He raised an eyebrow and glanced over again. "Don't lie, Ben. It's written all over your body that you're still cold." His glance roamed down over me and back to my face, and I felt heat race through me; it definitely wasn't from the van's heater. I also felt my cock stiffen in my jeans. I hadn't had that happen since I was younger. I felt like a teenager with no control over his urges. There was desire in his look, and my body couldn't help but react to it.

I cleared my throat. "Ah, you need to take a left down this next road," I said, distracting myself and him from whatever the hell was happening between us. He cleared his throat too and shifted in the driver's seat. I tried not to think about his reaction. I didn't want to dwell too much on the possibility that he liked me like I liked him. *That couldn't be true, could it?*

Rick followed my directions and went to the next place on the list. I pointed out the kids I was sending him over to and waited in the van as I watched him work his magic. He chatted, they laughed, he handed over supply packs, and within five minutes was back in the van. I had taken the liberty of moving into the driver's seat while he was out this time. It would be easier for me to drive for a while rather than have him do everything.

"Stealing my seat?" He laughed when he jumped in on the passenger side.

I shrugged with a smile. "I thought this might be easier than just sitting there looking pretty while you do the driving and running out in the cold."

He gave me that look up and down again, and I felt it everywhere. "But you do looking pretty so well." He smiled with a sideward glance.

Fuck. I started the van and pulled out again into traffic.

Another two hours were spent driving around London, covering as much ground as we could, seeing as many of the groups the charity was aware of as we could. By then, we were both cold and tired, and it was time to call it a night. I put the heating up as high as it would go and headed back to the garage at the charity's building.

I pulled into the van's parking spot and turned off the lights and engine. I sat there for a moment, not really wanting to get out and have the night finally end.

"Thank you for trusting me with this tonight." Rick smiled, looking over at me, his head still leaning back on the headrest where he had tried to make himself comfortable.

"Thank you for offering to come out with me. I couldn't have covered half as much ground without you." I smiled back.

"Does that mean I've got a job when I want to help out?" He laughed.

"Anytime."

Silence filled the space between us, and we just sat there.

I wanted to move closer to him. I wanted to touch him, but I didn't know what I was allowed to do and what I wasn't. Instead, we sat, caught somewhere in between doing nothing and doing something. I wasn't mistaken anymore; there was something there in return. Part of me longed to find out. Part of me was terrified he might dismiss it later as a horrible mistake or a cheap affair.

Jesus, why do I overthink these things?

"I should probably go," he said, still looking at me.

I couldn't look away. "It is late."

"Yeah, it is." Still, his gaze was fixed on mine.

I couldn't take it anymore. I looked away, pressed the button to release my seatbelt, and pulled the keys from the ignition as I got out. Rick followed. Once he'd closed the passenger door, I locked the van and headed over to my car. Rick's was parked right beside mine.

We paused again at the back of our respective vehicles. Our eyes locked again. "Thank you," I said. "I enjoyed being out with you this evening."

He moved a little towards me and leaned against my car. "I enjoyed being out with you too." He smiled. "I'd like to do it again if you'll let me?"

I smiled and leaned on my car, facing him. "Anytime. I mean that. It was really nice to have your company tonight."

A second later, his lips were against mine. I gasped against his mouth and opened mine to his demanding tongue. His kiss was hard and passionate. It poured warmth into my body and hardened my cock. His hands found my waist and pulled me against him, and my hands grabbed his arms, my body moulding to his. We stood there at the back of my car like a pair of teenagers snogging in a bike shed, overloaded with lust and hormones.

He pulled back from me, breathless, and stared at me. "Sorry. I just couldn't stop myself. I've wanted to do that since the instant I met you."

I was breathless and speechless. My mind was raising a million thoughts a second.

I just kissed a prince.

He said he wanted to do that, and since he first met me.

He was passionate as hell.

He was hard and pressed against me.

He was an impressive kisser, and he took my breath away.

I wanted more, but did he?

A car pulled into the garage, and both of us blushed, the moment broken, reality breaking back through.

"I should probably get back." He smiled and bit his lip, his eyes focusing on my mouth.

"Okay." I nodded. It wasn't what I wanted to say. I wanted to ask if he wanted to come back to mine. I wanted to see if he wanted a night cap. But this was a prince. This was the man who would one day be king of a whole other fucking country. Where did I think something like this would go? Was he suddenly going to be my boyfriend? Was I going to be his king? I didn't think so somehow. And what about Emma?

He smiled at me, leaned in, and briefly pressed his lips against mine, and then got into his car and left. I stood watching until he disappeared out of the garage. I ran my fingers over my lips and thought about what had just happened. A grin crept over my face, even though I knew this wouldn't go anywhere. We moved in two very different worlds, and I honestly didn't know how those would reconcile.

Chapter Fifteen
Rick

I'm NOT sure how I made it back to Hampshire in one piece. It felt like I was floating. I had given in finally and kissed him like every cell in me had wanted to, and it felt amazing. Every ounce of everything that had crossed my mind about him, and liked about him, and wanted him to know, had poured out between our lips.

Ideas were forming about seeing him again; I needed it. There was a deep desire to be in his presence. I wanted to see just what would happen between us. There had never before been an opportunity to experience the feelings I was having for Ben. I was positively walking on air. He had pulled me against him. I'd felt the hardness of his dick against me. There had clearly been a connection on his side too. A craving for more was brewing between us. I couldn't lie. There was a strong desire for it within me. There was definitely something glorious happening between us, and I didn't want to deny a second of it. I wanted to ride it out to the very end, all the while praying it never ended. We might not have moved in the same circles, but something had put us together, and I was damned if I was going to let it all go to hell now. It was going to be life-changing and amazing, I knew it.

I crawled into bed in the silence of the castle, my mind racing, my cock throbbing, my mouth stretched out in the biggest grin. I lay there in the darkness until my brain and body calmed down enough for sleep.

"What the fuck are you grinning about?" Hugo grumbled the next morning.

I shrugged. "Nothing. Am I smiling?"

Hugo shook his head with a groan. "Okay. I'm not playing that game, so tell me or stop fucking grinning like an idiot. It's too early for that shit."

I laughed. Hugo had never been a morning person, and this was the worst he had been for a while. "You didn't sleep, I take it."

He glared. "No. Some twat fucked off and wasn't back until the middle of the night, thinking he wasn't missed and was a sneaky bastard when he wasn't."

I snorted. "Sorry, mate." He glowered some more. "Okay... yes, I have something to grin about. I was out with Ben doing stuff in London for the charity last night. And, well, I might have kissed him."

Hugo stopped eating his toast mid-bite. "Might have?"

"Yes. I *might* have."

He rolled his eyes at me and smirked. "You're such a dick."

"That's Prince Dick to you, knobhead." I laughed and snatched his toast from his hand before walking off for a shower.

Chapter Sixteen
Ben

I'D BEEN QUITE distracted since the night in London with Rick. I thought about it, overanalysed it, and thought some more. I'd hoped to hear from him, but other than the odd text or two, there had been nothing significant. I didn't know if he regretted what happened, or if he just plain wasn't that into me after all.

I was a little surprised to have a text from him after that.

Hey, Ben. I was just wondering if you still needed some help with those flatpacks? R x

I stared at the screen at the R and the little 'x' after. Could that much value really be put on the inclusion of the twenty-third letter of the alphabet? *Dear God, why am I such an overthinker!* I hit reply.

Sure, I have a mountain of boxes in front of me right now. Are you doing anything today?

I thought about adding an 'x' of my own and decided against it. Rick's reply was fast.

Tell me where. I'll be there asap! =D

I replied that it was all at the half-way house, put my phone away, and set about occupying myself until he arrived.

Twenty-five minutes later, Rick was standing in front of me with a fuller beard and a grin.

"Hello, you."

"Hello yourself," I replied, unable to resist smiling back at him. "Ready to get some work done?"

"For you, anything." He winked at me. God, how much I wanted that to be true. About the charity, and about me. He was giving me that look that made it impossible to think straight, and now we had kissed, it just made me think of how good his lips felt against mine.

"Follow me." I smiled and walked to one of the bedrooms. Rick followed and stopped when he looked in.

"You have to build all of that?"

I laughed. "Yes. There's a set like this in every bedroom and we have twenty-four bedrooms. You said you were ready to tackle a mountain of boxes," I reminded him.

"Christ, you weren't joking about it being a mountain." He looked around the room in awe.

"Do you want a room to yourself, or do you want to work in a team of two?"

I had barely finished my question when he replied. "Two."

"Okay." I nodded and handed him a tool belt with all the usual tools hanging from it. "Then you'll be needing this." He glanced at it, hung it low on his hips, and grabbed the nearest box.

"Let's get on with this, then." He raised an eyebrow and smirked.

This man is going to be the death of me.

"FUCK!"

I winced. He had missed the nail and hit his finger with the hammer pretty damn hard.

"Shit! Let me see." I pulled his hand towards me and looked over his finger, making sure he hadn't broken the skin anywhere.

'It's fine, it's just throbbing," he grumbled.

I didn't think about it, I just put it in my mouth, a sort of half kiss, half suck, and when I pulled it out from between my lips, I looked at him. "Feeling better now?" I asked, blushing as I realised what I'd done. *Shit!*

His eyes were hooded and darkened with lust. "Yeah," he said softly. "Much better."

The pull that had been there that night against my car was back. I wanted to close the distance between us. I wanted to feel his lips on mine again, and just as I thought he was about to, Molly appeared around the corner.

"Boss, have you got the forms for..." She looked at us both and paused mid-question. "Sorry." She was about to turn and walk away. Rick glanced at me, his eyes wide.

"Molly!" I called after her. "It's okay. Forms for what?"

Rick held his injured finger up. "I'll just go and run my hammer injury under a cold tap for a minute." He smiled at her and quickly left the room.

"Boss."

"What forms, Molly?" I asked with a look that begged her not to ask about it or lecture me when I knew only too clearly what was happening.

She sighed in resignation. "The forms for the insurance for this place. I thought I had them, but apparently, I don't."

I thought about where they were and then told her they were probably in my bag in the main office in the building. It had been the first room we finished so we had somewhere to put our things and to work from while we were trying to get it all up and running.

"Be careful," she warned and walked out as Rick came back in with a wet paper towel around his finger.

"Everything okay?" he asked.

I nodded. "She suspects something. I can tell."

Rick smiled at me. "I'm pretty sure it would be obvious to anyone who sees how we look at each other."

I stared at him. Why was this so easy for him? Didn't he realise what was at stake? I shook my head. "Is your finger okay?"

He nodded, and we got back to work with the flat-pack furniture.

By late afternoon, Rick and I had the furniture in three of the bedrooms complete. "I'd like to come back and do this again tomorrow if you need the help." He smiled.

Damn right I would. "As long as you can spare the time, that would be great. Thank you."

He nodded. "I'll be here."

"Did you use the yard at the back to park here?"

He shook his head. "I'm just down the street a little."

"I'll walk you there." I wasn't ready to have him disappear again just yet. We walked out of the building in silence and slowly down the street to where Rick's borrowed car was parked. He stopped and turned to me when he reached it.

"Can we talk about what happened last time?" he asked.

I braced myself. Here came the talk about it being a mistake and how it wasn't what he wanted. I just nodded.

"I know it's not a very orthodox position to be in for you, but I liked what happened last time. I want it to happen again. I would love to do it right now if we weren't standing in the middle of a London street in broad daylight, and I don't mean that to sound like I'm ashamed of you. God, I could never be. I just have a very interesting relationship with the press, and I want you and I to have nothing but applause from them."

Was I hearing this right?

"You want more?" I absently blurted out.

"Shit. Have I got this all wrong? Do you not want that?" He leaned back against his car, almost injured by my outburst, and I could see him rethinking everything that had happened to see what he'd missed.

"Oh, Christ. I do. I didn't mean it like that, I'm just... You want more of me?"

He grinned. "God, yes, Ben. I want a lot more. You're stunning."

"So, tomorrow, then?" I smiled shyly at him.

"Definitely."

"I'll text you the details of how to get into the yard at the back instead of parking on the street."

He nodded, got into his car, and headed into the London traffic.

Chapter Seventeen
Rick

I GROANED when a stack of newspapers was dumped on my stomach while I was still half asleep.

"Your parents are going to hit the roof, Rick. Wake the fuck up!" Hugo growled.

Oh, for fuck's sake. What now?

I grumbled as I shifted myself into the seated position and started to look at the headlines on the tabloids in my lap.

"Prince Frederick seen sneaking into The Domino Trust's new children's home."

"New furniture in Thornbay Palace?"

"Who has inspired Prince Freddie to give his image a makeover?"

Below each of the headlines and stories was a collection of photos taken through the window looking into the building, and me coming and going outside. I hadn't told anyone but Hugo. Someone had told them where I would be.

"Shit. How the hell did this get out?"

Hugo was pacing the floor. "I don't know, but I didn't tell anyone where you were going."

"Nah, I trust you."

"Do you think Ben told anyone?" He stopped pacing in front of me to ask.

I shook my head. "No, I trust him as much as I trust you."

Hugo sighed. "Fuck. Thought you might say that. I'll look into it. They might just have been following you. It's been a while since you've been in the press for anything trashy. They might just have been digging."

I agreed.

"You need to get ready. You know what will be asked of you shortly."

I knew my mother and father would summon me for the Spanish Inquisition of what I was doing, and why, and who with. Just what I needed.

***

"Would you like to tell me what the bloody hell you think you've been doing, Freddie?" Pa barked. "Do I have to remind you that you are the future monarch of this country, and here you are, going out without telling anyone, without security, swanning about all over London by yourself!"

My mother was watching him carefully, as though she was waiting for his head to explode. "Bertie, calm down. For heaven's sake, think of your blood pressure."

"Blood pressure?!" he roared. "What the hell do you think all this is doing for my damn blood pressure?"

He had a point. I was high profile, and I was taking an enormous risk being out in public with no one knowing where I was, and with no security with me. But I wouldn't have been able to slip around like I had been with a security detail lurking in the shadows with me. I certainly didn't want to draw more attention to myself than I needed to. I wanted to stay reasonably anonymous for a change.

"Pa, I understand completely where you're coming from." I tried to soothe him before launching into my reasons as to why I had done it. "But I needed to do something that wasn't about the press getting to look at what I was doing. I just wanted to be one of the crowd; someone who wouldn't get a second glance when I was out and about."

He put his head in his hands and looked in despair at my mother. "Frederick, I know this might have escaped your attention, but you are the first in line to the throne. In today's climate, you may as well have a target on your back. Why, for the love of God, would you then make it easier for something to happen to you?"

I bowed my head, but I knew there was no point in arguing with him because there was nothing he was saying that wasn't true.

"Why did you do this, Frederick?" Mama asked, putting her hand over my father's as he sat beside her.

"I met Ben that first day at The Domino Trust. It's his family's charity and he's the director. We just hit it off, and I wanted to have a chance to see what the charity really does."

"And is there anything more to it? Do you have feelings for this man?" My mother was a very astute woman.

"Yes. I like him, Mama. I like him a lot. We have kissed, and he seems interested in me too."

My mother smiled warmly. My father looked at me like I'd just told him I'd sold my soul to the devil for a blow job. Knowing Pa, he probably thought that's exactly what I had done.

Mama squeezed his hand tighter. She could read him better than I could. "I know you understand the responsibilities of the family you have been born into, son. And I know you understand there are things that are expected of you, and rules you need to follow. But I trust your decision."

I stared at her. She was good. Very good. I was meant to think about all the things my family expected of me and reflect on how Ben would fit into that. She was making it all my choice, but not without applying the pressure to the decision she thought I should make, without the war, the hot-headed words, and demanding it of me. She just hadn't considered one thing. My feelings for Ben were not something I was about to give up on easily. He was someone I needed to have around, and they would eventually just have to get used to that fact. Social standing or not.

I nodded. "Thank you, Mama," I said, and ended the video call, leaving them 'discussing' their differences in opinion of the whole situation.

"So, how fucked are you?" Hugo laughed.

I gave him the middle finger and pulled my phone from my pocket. I glanced at the screen to see a message from Ben.

I know this might seem a little forward and premature, but I was wondering if you wanted to come to my house for dinner tomorrow night. I was also thinking that, given the newspapers today, it might make sense if you were to not help out tomorrow with the furniture building. If those photos had been

*when you hit your finger with the hammer the story
might have been different :o*

I hit reply.

*Agreed about the photos, and I would absolutely love
to. Where and when?*

A few minutes later, he texted me back his address and
told me to be there by eight. I was looking forward to seeing
him already.

Chapter Eighteen
Rick

I used my motorcycle to go to Ben's house. I knew there was a risk since the press knew what to look for, but I also figured that, since it had two wheels not four, it would be a lot easier to out-manoeuvre them if I needed to.

At five minutes to eight, I pulled into his drive and put my bike in his garage like he suggested, closing the door so my bike remained unseen. I knocked on his front door. I held my breath and waited. Moments later, Ben arrived at the door wearing an apron over his clothes and a grin on his face.

"Hello there. Come on in." He stepped aside so I could enter. I walked in to the hallway of Ben's charming Edwardian house in the London suburbs.

"Your house is gorgeous," I said as I looked around.

He grinned and walked down the hall to the back of the house. "Thank you. I'll give you a proper tour later, but for now, I'm back here in the kitchen." I followed him into a roomy open-plan kitchen and dining room, with the table set up to perfection. Perched at the other side of the kitchen island was Emma, colouring in.

"Hello, Prince Frederick." She grinned as I approached.

I sat beside her and grinned back. "Hello, Miss Emma. What are we colouring?"

She pushed her crayons in my direction and showed me what she was working on.

"That's beautiful. Can I help?" Emma nodded.

Ben turned to look at her. "Don't get too comfortable there, munchkin. You know you're going to bed in five minutes."

She looked like she was being inconvenienced instead of being told to sleep. Her little face scrunched up. "You know. If you like, you and your daddy can come out to my castle sometime and I can show you all the cool stuff there." I wasn't sure what a six-year-old would find cool about the castle, but it was an attempt to get along with this lovely little girl.

"Do you have suits of armour?" Her expression lit up instantly.

I nodded. "We do."

"Do you have horses?"

"We do."

Ben turned around to look at his daughter's expression. He rolled his eyes and smirked at me.

"Daddy, can we?" she asked in pure excitement.

Ben came around the kitchen island, closed Emma's colouring book, and put her crayons in the box. "I'm sure we can sort out something for you to see the castle, munchkin. Come on. Bedtime. Say goodnight to Rick."

"Goodnight, Rick." She sighed, resigning herself to the fact that it was her bedtime.

I smirked. "Goodnight, Miss Emma."

Ben scooped her up in his arms and headed off upstairs with her. A short while later, he returned.

I had looked around the kitchen in his absence. Ben had put in a hell of a lot of effort for me, and I was very impressed. The smells filling the room were amazing.

"Damn, that smells good." I grinned when he returned to checking on what he had cooking on the stove. "Anything I can do?"

Ben laughed. "Not this time. Get your ass over there and sit down. There's wine there on the table if you want to pour yourself some."

"Did she get to bed okay?" I asked and waved the wine bottle in Ben's direction to silently ask if he also wanted some.

Ben nodded. "Yes, please, and she did. She's very excited about visiting a real castle. Thank you for that. You didn't have to."

I smiled. "I would like you to come. Both of you. She's a wonderful kid, and I love her attitude." I poured him a large glassful, bringing it over to him as he cooked.

He laughed. "Yeah, she's something else, alright. But thank you. I appreciate it."

I slid my hands over his hips and snaked my arms around his waist, tucking my face in over his shoulder. "Anytime. Now, what are you making?" I asked, nuzzling against his neck.

"A burnt mess if you keep that shit up."

I dropped my hands from him and took a step back. Ben groaned at the loss of contact between us. I smirked, and he glanced at me over his shoulder. "You are trouble."

"Am I?" I laughed. A tea towel landed in my face, and I chuckled more as I made my way back to my seat at the dinner table. I watched as he moved around the space, juggling pots, pans, and utensils with effortless grace as he continued to cook whatever was making that amazing smell fill my nose. "What are you making?"

"Honey and Kashmiri Chilli Butter chicken, with basmati rice, and garlic and coriander naans."

This man was going to get to my heart through my stomach. "Damn, that's pretty much my favourite kind of comfort food. Do we have dessert?" I asked cheekily.

"Maybe." He smirked. He finished plating everything up and brought it all over to the table. He set the plate in front of me, and I got to see the masterpiece that was Ben's butter chicken curry.

"Wow. That looks amazing."

He was blushing again. "Thank you. I hope you like it."

"This happens to be my favourite. I'm going to love this." And as if to prove a point, I gathered some rice and curry onto my fork and popped it into my mouth. It was amazing. I moaned. "Jesus, Ben. This is fantastic," I said with my mouth still full. Ben looked very pleased with himself and tucked into his own plateful.

After dinner, we headed for the sofa, both of us well-fed and having enjoyed the wine and conversation. "Thank you for that meal. It was wonderful. *You* are wonderful."

His face flooded with colour. This was turning into something I liked seeing.

"You're sexy when you blush," I said, touching the spikes in his hair.

"I think you might be biased."

I shrugged. "I don't think so."

He leaned against my hand and closed his eyes. I leaned in and kissed him. At first, my lips were soft against his, gently asking permission and acceptance, and as he responded to me, I crushed my lips against his harder, my tongue sliding along his lips, begging for entrance.

The harder I kissed him, the more he responded, pushing back against me, his tongue rolling over mine as they tangled in our mouths. My cock started to stir in my jeans, and I moaned against his mouth. I pressed my body against his, encouraging him to lie back. Instead, Ben pushed back against me and moved until he was straddling my lap.

I grabbed his ass, feeling his hardness against mine. He wrapped his arms around my neck and took control of the situation, grinding against me, kissing me fiercely. I pulled back from his mouth. "Fuck, Ben."

"Good idea." He smiled and slammed his mouth against mine again. He rolled his hips, his cock rubbing against mine through our clothes. I needed more. He was igniting a fire within me, and I needed to have him naked. Again, he pulled his mouth from mine, leaned back, and took off his t-shirt, dropping it to the floor beside him.

I let my eyes roam over him. I couldn't resist feasting on all the flesh on display. I ran my hand over his chest, only the tiniest hint of hair covering it, his skin warm and soft under my fingertips. His fingers started on the buttons of my shirt. I sat there, stroking his skin, getting more and more turned on, letting him remove whatever clothing of mine he wanted to.

When he was done with the buttons, he flicked my shirt open, and his eyes fell upon my tattoo. His fingers, lightly tickling, traced the outline of the dragon on my chest. "Does it mean something?"

"Yes. It's duality. A dragon is a fierce beast that can destroy everything it comes into contact with with ease, and yet, it's also the symbol of wisdom, strength, and a force of good."

"Like you." He leaned over and kissed the head of the dragon resting on my left pec muscle.

"Like me," I agreed and pulled his mouth back to mine, kissing him hungrily.

We kissed and caressed for what felt like hours, teasing each other, grinding against each other, working ourselves into a frenzy that would only ever end one way. I felt guilty about that. I didn't want to rush this. I didn't want to come to his house and have him bouncing on my cock before the night was over. Well, I did. But not like this. This was rushed, and lust-fuelled, and I wanted to savour every single moment with him. I wanted Ben to know just how much I cherished him and wanted so much more for us than a fumble on his couch.

"Oh, God!" I panted as his mouth moved over my chest and he started to slide off my lap. I knew what was happening and where he was going, and, dear God, as much as I wanted the sweet release of his mouth right that minute, I knew I needed to stop him. I wasn't going to use him for a fumble and then leave. And I would have to leave. I couldn't stay in his house overnight. I would be missed, and that would start all manner of shit.

"You need to stop."

Ben looked up at me. "Don't you want…"

I cupped his face and stopped that thought instantly. "No, no, no. I do. Sweet Christ, I do. I want it so much I can't see straight, but I can't stay the night, Ben."

Ben looked at me. "That's okay."

I shook my head. "No, it's not. I'm not going to finally be with you, only to have to rush through it all and leave right after. I'm not using you like that. It's not right."

He smirked. "You can use me exactly like that any damn time you feel like it, Rick."

I groaned and kissed his lips softly, his face still cupped in my hands. "You are worth so much more than that. I will be taking you to bed, and soon, but not until I can work it out that we stay together, neither of us needing to run away anywhere. When I'm done with you, your limbs will be jelly, and you will need holding all night until you're ready for me to do it to you all over again."

That was a promise I intended to keep.

"Well, when you put it like that." He grinned. "You don't have to go yet, do you?"

I glanced at my watch. One a.m. Damn. I nodded. "Shortly. But I have thoroughly enjoyed this evening, and I think we need a lot more of it and soon."

He nodded and sank back down against my chest, his lips on my dragon again, creeping back towards my neck, and when his mouth finally found mine, I grabbed handfuls of his arse and made the most of the time I had left with him that evening.

Chapter Nineteen
Ben

It had been a week since Rick had left me frustrated that evening in my house, but I took comfort in the fact that I had left him just as frustrated. My phone chirped, and I glanced at the screen.

Do you like the theatre?

I smiled and replied.

It's been known. What do you have in mind?

My phone chirped again.

Well, a friend has a very exclusive box with a private entrance and everything. They have a show of La Boheme next week if you're interested?

That opera just happened to be one of my favourites.

I'll be there! Just let me know the details! x

He texted me back with the day and time and told me he would collect me from the charity offices beforehand. I grinned. I couldn't wait.

Hugo Everly was driving, and we were taken to the Royal Opera House, ushered in through the private entrance, and up into a secluded little box right on the edge of the left of the stage.

"This is amazing." I smiled at Rick.

"Have you been here before?"

I nodded. "Hell yes, but never up here in something as exclusive as a box."

His hand found mine, and he squeezed it with a grin. "You should always have the best of things, and if I can help it, I intend to make sure you get them."

He warmed my heart, and I leaned over and kissed his cheek gently. "Are you sure we won't be seen here?"

He nodded. I leaned over and kissed him again properly. "Thank you for this. It's already the best time I've had at an opera."

He beamed and held my hand tighter. "I'm glad."

We watch the story unfolding before us. Painter Marcello and poet Rodolfo, struggling artists trying to survive in 1830s Paris. Rick kept my hand in his throughout the whole of Act I. During the interval, we were treated to cocktails and nibbles. Rick was the perfect gentleman, asking about my day, sneaking me kisses when he could, holding my hand almost the entire time. My heart fluttered at his every touch. I was done for in the best possible way; I was falling for Rick, hard, fast, and without restraint. I could only hope he was experiencing the same feelings about me. I hoped that was the case, but I couldn't be sure.

Every time I looked at Rick in the second act, I found him already looking at me. His smile was so warm and genuine that I couldn't help but grin back at him.

When we arrived at the interval before Act III, he leaned over to talk to me quietly. "I have something I need to tell you." He squirmed a little, nervously. "I have to go on a state trip next week. It was sprung on me at the last minute, but it's only for a few days, and I'd like to see you again when I get back." He looked at me, waiting for my reply.

"Canada, wasn't it?" I smiled.

His brows creased. "You already knew?"

"It might have been on the news earlier." I chuckled.

He sighed. "I was worried you would think I was running away from you or something. I wish I could take you with me."

I stroked his cheek. "I have a job, and I can't just drop everything and go swanning off on a moment's notice, even if I was allowed to go with you."

"I'll be texting you every day."

"You'd better." I warned with a smile.

He looked at me with a lustful stare and kissed the back of my hand. "Just try and stop me."

Damn, he has such an effect on me.

Act III started, and we directed our attention back to the stage. This time, when I glanced over at Rick, I saw him staring at the stage, chewing a little on his bottom lip, his eyes glassy. The fate of Mimi played out before us, and my beautiful prince wore his heart on his sleeve as the tears spilled from his eyes.

The lights came back up and we got up to go. Before I

had a chance to register what was happening, my back was pressed against the wall of the box, and Rick's mouth was on mine, hot and demanding. I responded with the same fierceness and ran my hands through his hair, holding his head, keeping his lips pressed hard against mine.

"I just..." he breathed against my mouth when he finally came up for air.

I closed my eyes. "I know."

I understood, I really did. The feelings between us were rising, and we had just watched the most beautiful tragedy unfold before us. Neither of us wanted to think about losing the other, but with the ending of La Boheme, that was exactly the thought that had flashed through both our minds.

"I don't want to lose you either," I admitted, and I was rewarded with another fierce kiss before there was a knock on the box door and Hugo asked us if we were ready to leave.

Chapter Twenty
Rick

I WAS TEXTING Ben as I had promised before I even left the UK on my flight to Canada.

> *On the plane now. I miss you already. Can I take you out when I get back? Unless you have more work for me in the half-way house? ;)*

It wasn't long before he replied.

> *Thank God for this soon-to-be time difference. I might actually get some work done :-P And damn right I want to see you when you get back!*

I grinned at his message. *Cheeky shit.*

> *Oh, I'm sorry to be bothering you at work, sir!*

A few seconds later, my phone vibrated with another message from Ben.

So you should be. Who do you think you are, a prince or something? :-P

I snorted at that message and tapped out a reply.

Funny you should mention that. Better shove this on airplane mode. Course, if you had an iPhone not a Samsung, I would be able to iMessage you on the onboard Wi-Fi :P

I waited a moment before I turned off my cell coverage for a reply before we took off.

Well, I don't, so I will talk to you in 8hrs. Have a safe flight xx

I didn't say anything else to Ben, but I did text Hugo.

Do me a favour? Grab the new iPhone and take it over to Ben and make sure he sets it up.

Two hours into my flight, just as I was dozing off a little, my phone vibrated again.

Was this really necessary, you nutcase?

I laughed and hit reply.

Well, you didn't have an iPhone, did you?

I watched the '...' appear to tell me he was typing.

Well apparently, I do now, because my boyfriend thought it was necessary! You really didn't need to do this!

I grinned at the message and tapped out another reply.

Say that again ;D

Again, I waited.

Which part? That you're a nutcase?

I laughed.

No, the other part.

My boyfriend x

I grinned. There was something about him calling me that that just felt so good.

Yeah, that part. Damn, I like how that sounds!

Go and sleep or something, I have work to do! lol

Will do xx

And I tucked my phone back into my pocket and had a doze for the next few hours.

Five hours later, turbulence woke me. "Sorry about this, Your Highness." Clare grimaced.

I laughed. "You can't control the weather. Don't worry about it."

"The captain has asked that you keep your seatbelt fastened for now, Sir."

I nodded and gave my belt a bit of a tighten. Luckily for me, I had fallen asleep before being told I could take it off. I watched as Clare buckled herself into the flight crew seat and smiled.

For the next twenty minutes, the plane juddered, jumped, and bobbed its way through the air. Flying wasn't something that ever bothered me, but this was starting to make me feel a little queasy. I pulled my phone from my pocket and texted Ben.

We've hit turbulence. I think I'm going to be sick!

Within moments, I had a reply.

God, is it bad? I hate that part of flying!

I smiled.

Might be a good job you're not here with me then. It's been bumping along for at least fifteen minutes now. Still, I'm sure I could have distracted you. ;)

A little harmless flirting wouldn't hurt right now. It would distract me from the shaking the aircraft was doing.

Oh, is that so? And how would you be doing that exactly?

I grinned.

Well, I can think of a few places I might like to put my mouth.

I thought about how he would be blushing reading my message, and I pulled the blanket across my lap to hide how that thought was affecting me.

Damn, Rick. I'm at work, and now I can't get up from my desk for a while!

I snorted.

Funny, I've just pulled a blanket over my lap to hide what you're doing to me ;)

I watched the '...' again and waited.

Oh, yeah, that's helping... NOT! I have a meeting in 30 minutes, you sod!

I grinned and tapped a reply out quickly.

Then you should go and take care of that, and show me how you do it ;)

I was being forward, but I just couldn't help myself.

Prince Frederick, did you just ask me for a dick pic? :-O

He almost had me blushing.

Maybe ;)

I waited for the dots to appear, but they didn't, and I chuckled to myself at his amazing restraint and put my phone back in my pocket.

We had just landed in Ottawa when my phone vibrated in my pocket. I unlocked it and looked at the message Ben had sent. *Holy shit.* It was exactly what I had suggested. It was also the most perfect penis I had ever seen, and judging from the way he had his hand around it, it wasn't exactly small. I mean, I had felt the rough outline of it in our bumping and grinding, but I had yet to actually feel him up like that. Ben Roberts had a mighty fine cock. And now I had to face the Prime Minister of Canada with my own dick straining to get out of my trousers. *Shit.*

"Premier Minister Gagnon. Bonjour, c'est un plaisir d'être ici." I smiled as I set foot on the tarmac and shook his hand.

"Bonjour Votre Altesse, bienvenue au Canada." He bowed politely.

"Thank you. It's lovely to be here."

We stood conversing, allowing the press their moment. "I trust you had a good flight, Sir?"

I sighed. "A little bumpier than I would have liked, but I'm here now, and ready for a wonderful visit." I smiled politely.

Gagnon walked me over to the awaiting car, and soon I was heading for Rideau Hall.

The days passed uneventfully on this trip. Everything happened just as it should have, with everyone on their best behaviour and obeying protocol. To say I was relieved was an understatement. I just wanted to get back and see Ben again. In fact, I'd had an idea.

So, I've been thinking.

He replied quickly.

Not sure that's a good idea where you're concerned.

I glared at my phone with a smile.

I was going to ask you out on another date, but with a very special venue in mind.

Again, he replied almost instantly.

Oh, really? And where might that be?

I tapped my response and hit send.

Thornbay Palace, in the presence of the King and Queen.

The dots appeared, then disappeared, then appeared, then disappeared again. I replied again.

Ha! Ben Roberts is speechless. Someone mark that up in the history books. Don't worry, it will be informal, and it will be just the five of us.

The dots reappeared, and his simple message appeared on screen.

Five?

Well, I'm inviting you, and it would be rude if the invite didn't extend to Miss Emma too!

Again, I watched those three little dots appear and disappear over and over until, after about five minutes of typing and deleting, Ben finally replied.

Okay x :-o

I grinned. In a few hours, I would be back in the air and heading back to Ben. I thought about how easy it was to look at it like that. I didn't view it as going home. Or rather, I did, and Ben was that home.

Chapter Twenty-One
Ben

Panic had filled every part of me the closer it got to the day I was going to Thornbay Palace for dinner. At the very least this was me and my daughter getting on a plane and jetting off to a foreign country. It wasn't that I hadn't taken her on a plane before, but, this was to meet a king and queen, and I just prayed Emma and I would make the right impression. I had been to a few 'meet the parents' dates in my life, but this one had to be the biggest deal of all of them. This was terrifying on two levels. The first, this was the King and Queen of Solena. That was enough to make me shit my pants on any normal day. But secondly, these were my boyfriend's parents, and he wanted me to meet them. Meeting the parents was the stuff of myth, legend, and scary consequences; just ask Ben Stiller!

Rick and Hugo had both explained what was expected of me. I was understanding a lot about why Rick and Hugo got on so well. Hugo was lovely and welcoming of me, even if he did tease his best friend about it. I was getting the hang of all the rules. They gave me boundaries, but I could see why Rick would feel the need to rebel against them. For me, they were calming. For him, they were controlling.

Hugo arrived at my house with Rick to collect us. "Are you ready for the lion's den?" Hugo laughed.

Rick punched him in the arm. "What the hell is wrong with you? Dick. Don't say things like that!"

Hugo smirked at him. "Oi! Language!"

Rick looked sheepish, and I looked at Emma, who was chuckling. I touched Rick's arm. "I'm meant to be the nervous one here."

"I just... I really want them to like you. You're important to me."

Hugo chortled. I frowned, and he shook his head. "No, I don't mean it like that. It's just in thirty-four years he's never thought enough about anyone to bring them home to his parents. This is absolutely priceless for me. He's so easy to wind up about it." He snorted.

Rick glared.

"Let's get in the car, you two." I laughed.

I sat silently on the trip across London to the airport. Rick held my hand the whole way to reassure me. Hugo kept smiling in the rear-view mirror. When we pulled up outside the private hangar at the airport, driving straight through security and onto the tarmac, a medium-sized jet was waiting for us.

"Is that our plane, Daddy?" Emma looked up at me as we stood in front of it.

Rick smiled at her and held out his hand for her to hold. "It is, indeed, Miss Emma. Do you like it?"

She shook her head. "It's very small."

I felt heat creep into my face. My daughter was going to be my undoing.

"It is, but guess what?" Rick grinned at her, crouching down to her level on one knee. "The only people on the whole plane will be you, me, Daddy, and Hugo."

"No pilot?"

Hugo snorted.

I knew where this was going and took Emma's other hand. "There is a pilot, munchkin, and a nice person to help us on the plane if we would like anything. Rick means there are no other passengers. It's a whole plane *all* for us."

"Oh, that's cool. Can I tell my friends about this when I get back to school? Danielle didn't believe me when I said I was going to meet a king and queen."

Rick grinned and scooped her up in his arms. "Danielle is very silly, and you can tell her you met the King and Queen and flew on a plane with no one else on it, and that it was amazing. Want to come and see where the pilot sits?"

"Don't touch anything!" I warned as they walked off in the direction of the aircraft stairs.

Hugo smiled and took our bags from the boot. "Don't worry, they'll be fine." He handed the luggage to the on-tarmac staff, and then nudged my arm as he passed. "Let's go before those two get into any trouble."

I shook my head and made my way over to the same stairs Rick and Emma had disappeared up.

Several hours passed, and we had touched down in Thornbay and been taken to the palace. Rick had been lavishing Emma with attention, and she was lapping it up. She was in her element exploring a palace, being told about all the funny things Rick knew of in the history of his home.

Before long, our tour was over, and we were settling into one of the sixteen opulent guest apartments that made up the south wing of the palace. Hugo was going to be babysitting Emma while Rick and I headed to the grand dining room. I was sure I was going to be sick.

Rick smiled at me. "Ready?" he asked.

God. "As I'll ever be."

He smiled and reached for my hand. I kissed Emma's head, told her to behave for Hugo, and let Rick lead me out into the hallway.

I followed him silently, taking in the surroundings as he walked me through to where we were dining with his mother and father. I tried to keep the rules in my head, but also reminded myself that these were *just* my boyfriend's parents.

We walked into a room with a dining table set out for the four of us, and a few sofas by the fire as well. The King and Queen were already there with drinks, waiting by the fire.

"Pa, Mama, I would like to introduce you to Benjamin Roberts." They stood and turned to me, and I bowed as I knew I should.

Queen Helena held her hand out for me to shake. "Hello, Ben. It's lovely to meet you, and I'm very glad you could be here this evening."

I shook her hand with another small bow. "Thank you, Your Highness."

"I would be very honoured if you called me Queen Helena this evening. It's still a little stuffy, but it's better than Your Highness." She smiled warmly, and she reminded me a lot of her son.

I nodded. "Thank you, Queen Helena. That's very kind of you."

She glanced at the King and gave him a look that almost wasn't there. He puffed out a breath and held out his hand. "Benjamin," he said curtly.

I shook his hand too. "Your Majesty." I smiled nervously.

'Sorry,' Rick mouthed when I glanced over.

"Would you like a drink, Ben?" Rick asked.

"Yes, please." I nodded.

The Queen invited me to sit with her, and I paused until she was on the seat before parking my backside beside her. "So, you met Rick through the charity?" she asked.

"I did." I took the glass of wine Rick offered to me.

"You and the charity seem to have done him a great deal of good, my dear. My son wasn't the most settled person in the world, but the way he carries himself and how he is seen in the press these days has made a remarkable turnaround. If you're as much of a part in that as I think you are, then I would like to thank you."

I nodded. I was in awe, and heat crept over my face. "Thank you very much for saying so, Queen Helena, but I think your son may just have been misunderstood by the press for the sake of a story." I glanced over at Rick, and I knew from the look on his face that I was blushing and the effect it was having on him that I was saying nice things about him.

The King stood by the fire, making no comments at all, merely providing his presence for the evening. I suspected Queen Helena had told him to.

"Tell Mama about the half-way house," Rick prompted, and Her Highness turned to me, attentive to what I was about to say.

I explained about the work the charity did, and how we had come to have the half-way house. I told her about Rick helping out and everything he had done, and the goodness I saw in him, and before long, it was Rick who was blushing.

A member of their staff came into the room and stood by the side of the door, saying nothing. Queen Helena glanced in her direction after five minutes and announced that we should move to the table for dinner.

I waited for the King to move and be seated before I did the same. The same when the food arrived. I waited for him to start eating and watched for him to finish as protocol dictated. I didn't want to let Rick down in any way, and more than that, I really wanted his family to like me.

"We will have to introduce you to Rick's brother at the next garden party," his mother told me. I was amazed. I glanced at Rick, who was grinning. His mother liked me, and she liked me enough to offer me an invitation to meet more of his family. So far, the evening was a success.

Dinner was lovely; the Queen chatted, and the King watched. I felt like I was under extreme scrutiny; I was. "How did you come about this charity job you have, Benjamin?" the King asked.

I explained the charity's background, as I had to Rick before. I told His Majesty about my great-grandmother and the work she had done. I also told him she had been to Thornbay Palace herself at a garden party held by his grandfather, King Alexander. I explained that I had a master's degree in social work, and I had worked in a few different charities, learning all I could before taking over as director of The Domino Trust when my father had retired a few years ago.

The King nodded but didn't really say more beyond 'I see' or 'indeed'. I was worried I wasn't making the impression I should have been. When the evening ended, they both shook my hand, and the Queen told me she was looking forward to an informal luncheon tomorrow to meet Emma and insisted we were to come back to the garden party in the summer months. I bowed and exited the room with Rick and sighed in relief that the night was done.

Rick took me by the hand and pulled me into an alcove. His lips crushed against my mouth and his tongue slid out to find mine. He kissed me hard and left me breathless. "You were fucking amazing," he whispered against my lips.

I frowned. "I don't think the King likes me very much."

Rick shook his head. "No, you were brilliant, and you made the perfect impression on him. You'll have to trust me on that one, but you really did. Tonight couldn't have gone any better if we'd tried."

I smiled at him. "Do you really think so?"

He kissed me again. "I know so!" He grinned and led me hand in hand back to the south wing.

Chapter Twenty-Two
Rick

After how well the initial dinner with Ben had gone, I decided it really was time for me to take the plunge. I wanted more. I needed more. I had been the rebel prince, biting his thumb at all the palace rules for far too long. I was sitting with my mother for breakfast that morning to discuss it with her.

"Mama, you have always said there would always be a home for me in Hampshire at Odiham if I wanted it. Is that still the case?" I asked tentatively.

She nodded. "It's always been waiting for you, Frederick. Even if your choice is to make it your permanent residence, for now." She smiled. "Just don't move someone into it with you just yet." She chuckled.

I grinned and kissed her cheek. "Thank you, Mama. I wasn't going to, I promise. Not yet," I added with a wink.

"I know you have some of your belongings over there already, but get Hugo to arrange for the rest of your things to be moved. You can be over there permanently within the week."

I nodded, grabbed some toast from the plate in front of me, and headed off to find Hugo.

I have some news. Long story short, do you fancy having a housewarming dinner with me in my new place?

I texted Ben. I had told him I wanted to be able to stay the night with him and I meant it. But now it would make a lot more sense if he was the one staying with me instead.

Hugo was sitting having his own breakfast, reading a newspaper.

"I have a job for you."

He glanced up at me. "Right now?"

I grinned. "Well, maybe you can have your breakfast first. Maybe."

He rolled his eyes. "Here we go again. Go on, spit it out."

"We're moving."

He looked at me like I had grown an extra head. "Is that the royal we? And where might *we* be moving to?" he asked.

I sighed. "No, that's the actual we. You and me. We are taking up residence in Odiham Castle."

Hugo looked quizzical. "That building we've been living in for a few months now? I take it you mean permanently. Christ, it must be serious with your fella. Does this mean I could even see my way to picking up a nice girl and bringing her home?"

"Mate, if all goes well, you can have all the pussy over you want." I laughed.

He shook his head. "You're so vulgar. Where is your class?"

I glared.

Smirking, he replied, "I'm assuming the job part of it is that I have to arrange it and do all the shifting of your crap?"

I looked at him blankly. "Why have a dog and bark yourself?"

"Just for that, you can move your own shit," he said and got back to his breakfast.

My phone vibrated in my pocket.

Where are you moving to? And yes, you owe me a dinner you have cooked yourself. ;-)

A week later, I answered my *official* new front door to find Ben standing on my doorstep.

"This is gorgeous." He smiled and handed me the bottle of wine he had brought with him.

I stepped aside and let him come in. I set the bottle of wine on the end table in the hallway and took him by the hand. "Come on. Time for a tour before dinner." I smiled and pulled him along behind me up the stairs so I could show him the whole cottage.

Room after room, Ben was impressed with the castle I now called home, and we ended the tour in the kitchen. "Something smells good." He grinned at me.

I smirked. "You're not the only one who knows how to cook, you know."

"Is that so?" He laughed. "So, what are we having, then?"

"I'm making you a full roast dinner. A chicken," I informed him, and he nodded in approval. I poured him some of the wine I already had chilling in the fridge, and I kept working on the dinner that was almost ready.

"Are you making the gravy from scratch?" he asked, watching what I was doing. I grinned. "Oh, hell, Rick. Even I don't do that!" He laughed. "I'm definitely impressed."

"Good." I grinned and waggled my eyebrows at him. He chuckled at me, and I told him to go and sit at the table, just as he had with me. He sat, watching me intently as I finished serving up our roast chicken dinner. I set it on the table in front of him and set the gravy boat on the table too.

"This all looks fucking amazing, and the smell is divine, Rick."

"I hope you're saying the same when you taste it." I laughed.

Ben took that as a challenge and tucked in. "Jesus!" he announced with his mouth full. "This is to die for!"

I beamed with pride. I wanted him to know I wasn't just a prince, that I was a man. That I could cook, paint, build furniture... love.

We drank the bottle of wine, we ate all the food, and we retired to the sitting room. I put my iPhone into the speaker dock and put on my favourite playlist before plonking myself back down on the sofa beside Ben.

His eyes were closed, and he was humming along to the song that was playing. He looked so comfortable; he fitted in with this house perfectly. I wanted him to stay here. I thought about my mother's comment about him moving in with me, and I thought it was a pretty damn good idea.

"You're staring." He laughed and opened his eyes.

I snorted. *Busted.* "I wasn't."

He shook his head with a chuckle.

"Well, maybe a little," I admitted.

He looked over at me, serenity on his beautiful face. "This has been lovely. Thank you for inviting me."

I moved closer. "It's not over yet." I smiled and closed the space between us until my lips were against his. Our kiss started slowly, our tongues lazily lapping over each other's. He moved his body a little more towards me and his hand found my knee, sliding slowly up my thigh with a firm pressure that made my cock hard almost instantly. I moaned against his lips when his hand cupped my cock through my jeans and his tongue plundered my mouth.

My hand went to his face, holding his mouth against mine. I needed more. I needed to do what this had been building up to for so long, but I had promised I would savour it as much as I could, and even if it killed me, I was going to try. I moaned again with a gasp as he palmed my cock with the absolute perfect amount of pressure. "We have all night, you know," I breathed against his mouth.

"You've had me waiting too fucking long, Rick. I need this, and I need it now. Sod the savouring. You can do that the second time."

Second time. Fuck, yes. I moaned again and crushed my mouth on his, pulling him against me, encouraging him into my lap just as he had been when we were in his house that night. I grabbed his arse and pulled his hard cock firmly against my own. I needed him naked. I needed to feel my cock sliding inside him. I wanted it more than I wanted air.

I watched as he stripped off his t-shirt, and I pulled him against me so his nipples came towards my mouth. I sucked one of them between my lips, pulling on it, running my tongue over it. Ben moaned and shifted his hips against me, looking for the friction he needed against his dick.

I let go of his nipple and moved forward with him, pulling my own t-shirt over my head and discarding it on the sofa beside me. I ran my hands over his skin and down below the waistband of his jeans. When I cupped his cock, he hissed and moved against my hand.

"Tell me what you want," I panted.

He groaned and moved against my hand, licking his lips. "Say it."

"You," he moaned.

I grinned. "Where do you want me?" I asked, giving him a moment of firm pressure against his cock and encouraging a pleasure-filled sigh from him.

"Fuck!" He hissed when I moved my hand away. "Inside me, Rick. I need you inside me."

Fuck, yes. That was just what I was waiting for. I pushed him back off me, making him stand, undid my jeans, and slid everything to the floor. He stared down at my cock, his eyes hooded with lust, and undid his own jeans, discarding them to the floor with mine.

He dropped to his knees in front of me and wrapped his mouth around my cock, getting me nice and wet. I moaned and fisted my hand in his hair, thrusting up to meet his mouth. I was on sensation overload. Lust was driving me crazy, and I needed more.

"Ben, I don't want to come in your mouth as our first time!" I warned as he expertly worked over my length, driving me closer and closer to the brink, getting my cock wetter and slicker with every movement.

He stopped and moved back into my lap, and I held up my cock, readying it for his gorgeous arse. He looked at me, keeping my gaze as he slowly lowered himself onto me. He pushed down on me, and I felt his arse resist for a moment before giving way and letting me further inside him. His eyes were locked on mine as he teasingly lowered himself little by little onto my cock until my entire rock-hard length was buried deep inside him.

When he had me where he wanted me, he leaned in and kissed me hard. I couldn't resist it anymore. I slid my hands up his thighs, settling on his hips and I used my grip to move him up and down on me, letting me slide in and out of his beautiful arse. He moaned when I slammed him down on me after the third stroke; I couldn't control myself. I didn't want to. I needed to fuck him. I needed to fill him and make sure he knew he was mine.

The last few sex-starved few months came to a head, bubbling up between us as we moaned, and grunted, and fucked hard, Ben's hand stroking his own cock as his asshole stroked mine to perfection. We were frantic. We weren't making love like we had initially promised, we were fucking hard with an animalistic need. I had never needed anyone the way I needed Ben.

I love him.

I needed him to know how much I wanted him in my life, and how much he meant to me, so I showed it in everything I had to give to him in that moment.

"I'm going to come," I warned him. We had been careless, and I hadn't put a condom on in my lusty fog.

"Do it," he panted, rocking his hips on me in encouragement.

I didn't need any more persuasion. "Oh, fuck, yes. I'm going to come inside you." I groaned, grabbing his hips and slamming my cock hard into him as he stroked himself. Watching him touching his cock because of me was too much, and I growled out as the first spurts of hot cum sprayed out deep inside Ben. His orgasm followed within seconds, sending ribbons of jizz shooting over my chest and stomach. I ran a finger over it as it lay on my skin and sucked the digit clean right after.

"Oh, Jesus," Ben breathed, collapsing onto me, spreading his spunk over us both. He kissed me softly and nuzzled against my neck, exhausted from our union. I stroked his back softly as we lay there, still connected, my softening cock still where it had been. Slowly, we came back down to earth in a glorious, blissful bubble.

Chapter Twenty-Three
Ben

AFTER OUR INTENSE coming together in the lounge, we took ourselves to the bedroom and the same thing happened again, only this time, as I had suggested, we took our time and savoured every last second of it as we made love. There was a level of intimacy with Rick I had never experienced with anyone else. I felt loved. I felt cherished, and I felt every ounce of emotion he had for me.

We fell asleep in each other's arms, and it was there I found myself still when I woke up. I lay looking at Rick as he slept. A smile crept over my face, and I felt nothing but love. My stomach growled, and I tried to extract myself from Rick's hold. Luckily, or unluckily depending on how you wanted to look at it, he moved away from me, rolling onto his other side and letting me go.

I let my eyes roam over his glorious naked form one more time and got up carefully so as not to disturb him before I changed my mind. I pulled on my boxers and headed back downstairs to the kitchen.

I looked around and made myself familiar with Rick's kitchen, and then I hunted through his fridge to see what I could find. Fortunately, the Prince had a very well-stocked larder, and I found everything I needed for a full English breakfast. I put the kettle on, found a frying pan, and got to work.

I didn't notice Rick was behind me until he spoke.

"Well, this is a sight I could get used to in my kitchen." He grinned and strode over to me, his hands finding my waist again, his lips against the back of my shoulder. "Also, whatever the hell you're making smells incredible. I could smell it upstairs. It's what brought me down here."

"I'm just making some breakfast." I grinned at him, nudging him with my hip so I could get on with the cooking.

"Well, you do that, and I'll set the table," he said, taking my hint and moving back to let me cook. He sat watching me once the table was set. "You really do look like you belong in my house."

"Is that an open invitation?" I smiled and set a plateful of bacon, sausage, eggs, and toast in front of him.

"Might be. Depends if I can keep you barefoot and in the kitchen." He smirked, and I threw the tea towel at him. His laughter filled the kitchen, and I was pretty sure this was the only place I would want to be for quite some time. In Rick's company.

We ate breakfast, we chatted, and we cleared up the kitchen afterwards. Rick suggested we clean up ourselves and took my hand to lead me back upstairs and into his bathroom. His mouth was on mine in a moment, possessive and needy. He put my backside on the edge of the marble counter and knelt before me. "Rick, what are you... oh!" My question was interrupted by his hands tugging down the front of my boxers and freeing my hardening cock from beneath them, then running his tongue over my exposed skin.

Now, this is how to start a day.

His mouth encouraged my cock to harden further, and he slipped his lips around the head and slid down until I touched the back of his throat. Sweet Christ. I couldn't resist the warmth of his mouth. I fisted my hand in his hair and helped him to set the pace as he pleasured me between his lips. He was damn talented with his mouth and, before long, I felt that tell-tale tightness in my balls.

"Jesus, Rick. I'm going to come," I warned him, looking down. I tried to pull back, but he just grabbed my hips, looked up at me, and held me still as he took all of me deep in his mouth and I erupted down his throat. He kept looking at me as he licked and sucked the last of my cum from me before standing and kissing me hard, the taste of me on his tongue.

"You taste amazing." He smiled and turned on the water in the large shower, stripping off as the water warmed for us. "Coming in?" He grinned and took me by the hand to lead me into the shower.

He positioned me underneath the water, took a handful of his shower gel, and started to wash me, his hands slippery and running over every exposed inch of my skin. I moaned softly at the sensations. "Rick," I pleaded.

"Shh," he breathed against the small of my back as he stooped low to run his hands over my legs. Every single inch of my body was caressed by his hands. Every single nerve in my body was set on fire.

I tried to turn to reciprocate his actions, and instead, he pressed my hands against the cool tiles in front of us. "Don't move." He kissed my shoulder and pushed his knees between my legs, encouraging me to spread them wider. His soapy hands slid over my arse, between my buttocks, and made sure everything was as slippery as possible. I knew what was coming next. I could feel his hard cock press against the crack of my arse when he reached his hands around to the front of me, rubbing over my chest. He rubbed himself up and down in the suds of his shower gel before backing away from me the tiniest bit, reaching between us, and moving his dick to my arsehole.

I groaned at the sensation of him again and waited as he slid the head of his hard cock into me. He felt so good. I didn't think I would ever be able to get enough of having him right where he was at that moment.

"Rick," I pleaded again.

He kissed my back, gripped my hips, and thrust hard into me. My husky moan echoed in the shower around us as he did, and without giving me a moment to catch my breath, Rick started a demanding rhythm. Over and over, he slid in and out of my arse.

"God, Ben, you feel so damn good around my cock." He groaned as he pulled back, only to fill me completely once again. He held my hips and used that hold to withdraw and then slide back in as deep as he could. Time fell away as he held me there for what felt like hours, taking pleasure from me.

"Fuck, I love your cock inside me." I sighed.

"I need to put it there. Jesus, it feels fucking incredible."

I could feel his body tighten behind mine, and I knew he was getting close. I wanted him to lose control and fill me again.

"Fuck me, Rick. Fill me with your spunk."

It was all the encouragement he needed. He roared out as he pumped his cum deep inside me. I don't know how he stopped himself from collapsing to the floor after such a fierce orgasm. My legs felt weak and I hadn't been the one doing all the work. I turned towards him, kissed him tenderly, and I finally returned his sweet sentiment by washing him all over.

"I'm sorry I have to leave," I said, kissing him softly again, dragging out the process of leaving as long as I could.

"I wish you could stay." He smiled glumly.

"Next time, I'll bring an overnight bag or something."

He grinned. "I love that there will be a next time."

"I love that you want there to be a next time."

"I love that you cook for me." He grinned.

"I love that you let me stay."

He smiled and kissed me softly. "I love you. Of course I'll let you stay."

Warmth washed over me. *He didn't just say that, did he?* I looked at him, calmness on his face.

"Care to say that first part again?" I teased.

"You heard me."

"Maybe. Want to remind me anyway, just in case?"

He pulled me against him until his forehead was against mine, his eyes closed, and he breathed out against my mouth. "I love you."

"I love you too," I replied, and his mouth was crushed against mine until we parted breathlessly. "I still have to go."

"I know."

I kissed him sweetly one last time and headed back to where my car was parked so I could get home, get changed, and make my way to the office.

Chapter Twenty-Four
Rick

"I'M DELIGHTED FOR YOU, mate, because no one deserves this more than you do." Hugo grinned and hugged me with a manly slap on the back. "So, what are you going to do?"

I shook my head. I didn't have an answer to that question. "I need to talk to them about it, but I have no idea what they'll say."

He raised an eyebrow at me. "Really? No idea, huh?"

I sighed. He was right, as usual. Who was I kidding? They were going to go insane. They had been just about tolerant of us dating, but I think they hoped this was just a crush or a silly affair that would fizzle out in time. It was exactly why Ben was the only boyfriend I had ever brought home to meet them. A point which seemed to have been a little lost on them. They'd never met a boyfriend of mine until now. Surely that would have let them know exactly what I was thinking about Ben.

"I don't know what to do and what to say."

"But you love him, right?"

I sighed with a smile. "I do."

"Maybe that's a good point to start with?"

I shrugged. It was a fair point. My mother might be a little more receptive to that. My father, on the other hand, not so much.

"I think I'm going to ask for consent," I said, taking a deep breath and breathing it out slowly, trying not to think too much about the significance of such a request.

"An Instrument for Consent?" Hugo grinned. "You and he are a good match, mate. You're great with his kid and it makes me happy to see you so happy. But marriage? Is that really where you want this to go?"

I nodded. There was nothing to think about with this. Since the moment I had seen Ben, there was something about him. Some bizarre pull that made me need to be in his company. If I had to put a label on it, I would say it was like my soul finding and recognising in Ben that its other half lay within him. Not that I believed in that kind of thing. Obviously.

Hugo pulled me in against him in a hug. "I'm happy for you, and anything you need from me, you have it."

"Thanks, mate," I said, hugging him back.

"Want me to go and call the Lord Chamberlain and tell him you would like a video call with the King and Queen?"

"No, I think this is definitely the kind of thing that needs to be done in person, don't you? Can you arrange for the plane tomorrow? I just need to take care of a couple of things before we go. Can you call Finchbury Square and see if the Prime Minister can spare half an hour for a meeting with the future King of Solena?"

Hugo shook his head with a smile and walked off, lifting out his phone and scrolling through the contacts.

I needed to talk to Ben before I went. I texted him and asked him if he and Emma would like to have the day off and do some things in London. That I was heading home as something important had come up, and I wanted some time with him before I went.

Should I be worried?

I texted him back immediately to alleviate his concern.

Not one bit! Just family crap. I'll be back in a day or so!

His reply was short and sweet, and I knew he didn't buy my comment any more than I did. This was going to be a huge thing I was asking of the family. And a huge thing I was asking of Ben too. We hadn't been together very long, after all. Plus, there was his daughter to think about. It was the strangest thing. As rushed as this all was, there was nothing that made me want to stop. Nothing that made me think this wasn't a good idea.

Four hours later, Emma, Ben, and I were in a pod on the London Eye with a picnic. "Is this a princess picnic?" Emma asked.

I grinned at her. "Do you think it's fit for a princess?"

She frowned, carefully thinking about my question.

"If only there was a princess here to ask..." I grinned at her little scrunched face. "Do you think you could be a princess, Miss Emma?"

Her face lit up into a huge grin. "Yes! I could be a princess. I have a crown at home, don't I, Daddy?" She looked over her shoulder at Ben, waiting for him to confirm what she was saying.

He rolled his eyes ever so slightly, and I knew that meant a crown wasn't all Emma had at home. I was betting she had some dressing up princess gowns, tiaras, jewellery, and God only knew what else. "Yes, munchkin, you do."

Emma nodded to me. "Do you think I would be a good princess, Rick?" she asked as she shoved part of her sandwich into her mouth.

I chuckled. "Yes, I think you would make a very good princess. You have such lovely manners."

A sandwichy grin appeared again. She was happy with my answer.

"Daddy, how do you get to be a princess?"

"Well... uh...."

I interrupted. "You have to marry a prince." I smiled at her. "Or you could have Daddy marry a prince."

Ben stared at me. I could see it written on his face. Was I really asking him, or was I just putting it out there?

"Are you going to marry Rick, Daddy?"

Wow. She was right in there with the very question I didn't want to ask, and I wasn't sure Ben was ready to answer. "What if I got a nice prince for you, Emma?" I asked her, steering both of us back into the not as scary path of my proposal.

"Yuck!" she stated instantly. "I don't like boys; they don't let me play football. They say girls aren't allowed. They say girls aren't good at kicking the ball."

Well, that was that decided, then. Ben and I chuckled at her comment and looked nervously at each other, wondering what the other was thinking about the elephant firmly in the pod.

The rest of the day passed with boat rides in the park, ice creams, and fun together, just the three of us. When we got back to Ben's house, Emma was asleep, and I carried her in from the car and up to her bedroom. I waited as Ben changed her into her PJs still asleep and tucked her in. He smiled at her sleeping form as he turned the light off and turned to me.

"What's that look?" He smiled at me.

I smiled back warmly. "Oh, nothing. Just thinking that I've really enjoyed the time with you and Emma today. And that you're a pretty amazing parent."

"You'd make a pretty impressive parent yourself sometime. You handle Emma really well, and she can be a handful."

I let that idea wash over me. I was starting to like the idea of being a parent, and the idea of being Emma's other parent was just as appealing.

"Coffee? Wine?" Ben asked before heading back downstairs.

I had to return to the castle shortly, ready for my trip home tomorrow. Hugo had texted during the day to confirm he had sorted everything, and the plane was leaving at ten a.m. "Coffee wouldn't go amiss. I'll have to go back soon."

Ben made his way to the kitchen, and I followed him, making myself at home at his breakfast bar.

"Am I being too nosy if I ask what you have to go home for?"

I shook my head. "Not at all. It's just something I need

to talk to them about, and I thought it might make the most sense to talk to them about it in person."

"Something serious, huh?"

I nodded. "Something like that."

"You know you're making me nervous."

I frowned. "Why would you be nervous?"

"What if it's something bad?"

I moved around the island, and I wrapped my arms around him. "It's nothing bad," I said, looking at him, keeping eye contact so he knew I wasn't trying to hide something from him.

He sighed and kissed me; a soft yet passionate kiss. "I believe you. This is just very new for me, and kind of terrifying!"

Now I was the one who was uneasy. "Terrifying?" I asked, trying not to be too alarmed.

"Rick, you're a prince. Not only are you a prince, but you're also the next in line for the throne, a throne that isn't in England. You don't think that has led me to consider the fact that, someday, this is all going to end? I mean, I can't see there being another way in this. I'm tied to the trust, you're tied to the throne, and eventually, that will mean it will all go a certain way, don't you think?"

I was floored. Was that what he really thought was going to happen between us. Did he really think I could just walk away? And if that was what he thought was going to happen, why was he still with me? Why was he still allowing me to enter his life and into his family?

"Is that what you really think?"

He shook his head. "It's not what I want to happen, but I'd be lying if I said it hadn't crossed my mind."

Suddenly, I didn't know what to say to him anymore. I wasn't sure how to process what he was telling me. It had never occurred to me that he might think this would *not* continue. I guess because it had never occurred to me that it would end. I certainly didn't want it to.

"I'm sorry if that has upset you." He smiled regretfully, taking my hand in his. "I guess Emma's comment today just put me on edge. I don't think it's sensible to think about things I know won't happen."

I squeezed his hand a little bit tighter. I wanted to tell him there and then that it could happen, and it would be happening because I wanted nothing more. But I also knew I needed to talk to my family first so that, when I did ask Ben to marry me, and I *would* be asking him, it needed to be right. The setting needed to be perfect, and this wasn't it.

"I understand, and I guess the only thing I can really do is prove you wrong. Things like this, like you and me, these things are worth fighting for. They're worth finding a way for."

I hugged him tightly. I kissed him softly and an uneasy silence fell over us. Ben finished making the coffee and we sat chatting about absolutely nothing of importance, and then I said goodnight and headed back to the castle.

I was a little disappointed. I wondered if my plan would really work. I wondered what I would do if my parents didn't agree. I just hoped getting my mother onside would be enough.

"Are you sure you're okay? You have been silent since you got home last night," Hugo questioned with concern.

I sighed. I didn't know the answer to that question. I didn't know how to tell him about what had happened the night before and the things Ben had said. I wasn't entirely convinced that he wouldn't try to tell me what a bad idea it was in light of that.

Something inside me told me it wasn't a bad idea. I wouldn't let it be because I wanted him, no matter what it took for it to work out between us. I spent the rest of the flight in silence.

Chapter Twenty-Five
Rick

"You really love him, don't you?" Mama asked.

I grinned. "I do."

"It shows. You light up when you're talking about him, and your previous problems with the press seem to have all but disappeared." She smiled warmly at me. I thought about what she said, and I had to admit she was probably right. Ben seemed to be a settling influence in my life. He was fun to be around, but he also kept me grounded. He was just what I needed.

"He keeps me centred, and a little more rational about things, I think. I also think I might want to make things a little more official."

My mother was smiling. My father was not.

"What do you mean by official?" he asked.

"Well, I have an appointment to talk to the Prime Minister about how he thinks the opinion would go if I was to announce my engagement. I would like to ask your permission to get married, Pa. I want to ask Ben to marry me."

My mother beamed with happiness. My father frowned.

"Do you really think that's necessary?"

"You mean asking your permission? I don't, but it's the law, and the tradition, so it's what I'm stuck with." I was being cheeky; I didn't want to have to come cap in hand. I didn't care if the Prime Minister thought it was a bad or good idea. I just wanted to do what normal people in love did.

"Don't be flippant, Frederick!" my father scolded. "You know exactly what I mean. Do you really think you need to get married to this man?"

I shrugged. "Did you ask this of Alex when he wanted to get married? Was he given the third degree as to why it was necessary that he wanted to commit his life to the person he was in love with? Or was it more the fact that, because he was getting himself a wife and not a husband, you didn't even bat an eyelid at it and you just granted him permission?"

"Your brother wasn't looking for my permission to marry a commoner who already has a child."

"Oh, so it's the fact that he's common and a single dad, and not the fact that I'm gay that's the issue here, is it?"

"Frederick," my mother warned.

I glanced in her direction. I wasn't wrong and she could see that. My father had to recognise it too. "I'm sorry, Mama, but I know it's true, and you have to acknowledge it, and Pa, you must as well."

"That is not why I am asking about it and you know it. You being gay has always been openly accepted by this family. Your bother married a duchess. You want to marry the head of a children's charity with no family connections at all. He's a bloody foreigner too! Not to mention this is the first person you have ever shown an interest in and now you already think you want to get married?"

I couldn't believe this was a conversation I was having.

"Alex found a duchess through sheer chance. How many gay earls have been at any of the parties we have attended, Pa? I am thirty-four years old, and you're right, I haven't felt like this for someone before, but I feel it now. I want to have Ben in my life, and I want to have him there for the rest of my life. He makes me want to be a better man, and you keep telling me that's exactly what I need to do."

There was a knock on the door, and Hugo's head appeared around it. "Rick, the car is here." I nodded to him, and he disappeared again and closed the door.

I looked at my father, my hands clasped together as though praying to him. "Please, Pa. Just think about this. Having your permission would mean everything to me. I love Ben and I want to spend the rest of my life with him."

My father said nothing, and my mother gave me an apologetic look. I got up from the seat and left the room.

"Judging from the look on your face, it's not going well," Hugo commented. I glared at him. "Oh-kay then! Let's get you to the car and you can go talk to the arsehole Prime Minister."

"Oh, Your Highness. So lovely to see you again. What can I do for you?" Philip Montjoy, the Prime Minister, greeted me with a smile. He nodded to Hugo, acknowledging his presence.

I sighed. Time to pay the piper and call the tune. "I'm here today on personal business of a sort. I have already had a discussion with my father, and I have asked for his permission to marry. I would just like to discuss what you think the view from the country, and obviously the government, would be about this?"

Montjoy's eyebrows rose for a split second. He tried to correct his shock, but unfortunately, I had already noticed. "Your Highness is planning to get married?"

I wanted to groan. "Yes, Prime Minister." I glanced over at Hugo to see every muscle in his body was just as tight as mine. He wasn't impressed with Montjoy either.

"And His Majesty has agreed to this?"

He had better be kidding me. I could feel my anger rising. "My father will be offering an Instrument of Consent, but I thought it would be only right to make you aware of what will be happening." I was bluffing, but there was no way for Montjoy to know that. "Do you think the public will think favourably of a Royal wedding given the obvious circumstances?"

"Which circumstances do you mean?" he asked with a smirk.

Hugo flinched. I was beginning to understand why his popularity was down in all the opinion polls. He was more than a bit of a wanker. "I mean the fact that I'm gay. I mean the fact that this would be the first Royal gay wedding, and of course, adding to that there is the fact this is a foreign commoner." I was trying to keep my temper, but if he kept this up, I wouldn't be able to.

He stared. "Oh, *that* situation."

I inwardly started counting to ten. "Yes." I could see Hugo balling his fist out of the corner of my eye.

"I'm not sure how the country would feel about this, to be honest. There are still a lot of people out there who don't agree with that kind of thing. Now, I'm not one of those people."

Yeah, right. Sure he wasn't. Bigoted tosser. As if I wasn't aware of the fact that he had openly been on the 'No' campaign when the rights to gay marriage were voted on.

"Right, so you don't think the nation can be open to a gay marriage of a future monarch? Is that what you're saying?"

Montjoy scoffed. "Well, Your Highness, I don't know if I would go that far. I mean, this isn't a simple matter. The country might well have reservations on both counts. He's not from a noble family, not to mention he's not even Solenian, and then there is the whole situation of homosexuality as well. *People* might not like it."

People? I couldn't keep my anger in anymore. "I have to admit, Prime Minister, if people think in the same way as you, then I'm really not sure I care. I don't give a shit about this country thinking it can dictate what's good for me in my life. It's no one's damn business." I stood.

"Have you considered what you will do if the *people* kick up enough fuss and don't want you as their king because of *this*?"

I stared him down. "Yes. Then I'll fucking abdicate." With that, I was done. This conversation was over; I had said what I wanted and heard all I was willing to hear from this moron. I stormed to the door, Hugo anticipating my every move and already at the door to open it for me. My blood was boiling. I said nothing. I didn't look at anyone, I just moved through the building to the front door and got back into my car. Hugo got in beside me.

"Breathe."

I exploded. "What the fuck is wrong with that useless sack of shit? Just because he doesn't agree with it, no one else can be happy and he's not prepared to show any interest in supporting it?"

Hugo sighed. "You knew he wasn't going to be accommodating."

"I did, but you know what, Hugo? I didn't think he was going to be a complete wanker about it."

He laughed. "Philip Montjoy, conservative, backward thinking, misogynistic, homophobic, Modern Traditionalist Party chief tosspot, and you think he's not going to be an utter arsehole? Do you not remember we were in boarding school with his son, Lyle?"

I thought about it. Actually, I did remember Lyle. The shady little prick gave me a blow job in the library annex when we were sixteen. I smirked thinking about it.

Hugo grinned. "Yeah, *now* you remember him, right?" He paused, letting me think about it. "And now you also understand why daddy dearest is so against it all. He would have to acknowledge that sonny boy is a raging homo."

"Fucker," I grumbled. This day had not gone to plan at all.

Chapter Twenty-Six
Rick

IF I THOUGHT the day before had gone badly and it couldn't get any worse, I was wrong. So very wrong. Hugo stormed into my bedroom that morning and slapped my arse to wake me and give me the bad news.

"It was leaked!" he growled, shoving a copy of the most well-known tabloid under my nose. "There was no one in that fucking room other than you, me, and him, and yet here it is, all over the front page of this fucking trash rag."

I rubbed my eyes and looked down at what I was meant to be paying attention to. There in big bold letters was the headline.

"Prince Freddie to abdicate for foreign lover. He doesn't 'give a s!t about this country' - more on page 2".*

"Oh, fuck. Pa is going to go mental." I dropped the paper into my lap and ran my hands through my hair. "This can't be fucking happening." I heard the commotion outside my private quarters. I knew what was coming before it stormed into my room.

"Would you care to explain what the devil this horseshit on the front of that tripe of a newspaper is?!" my father bellowed at me.

"It's lies!"

"So, you didn't say it?"

"Not like that!"

Pa started to pace the room. "Not like that... Not like that... Freddie, if I had my way, I would be taking you outside to be horsewhipped. What the hell is wrong with you, boy? Why would you say anything like that at all to someone like him?"

Hugo coughed. "Your Majesty, if I may..."

Pa turned on his heel and stared at Hugo. "If you may what, Everly?" he snarled.

"His Highness didn't say what has been quoted, and even if he had, there were three people in the room at the time. There is a severe leak in Finchbury Square for this to have appeared at all."

My father listened to what Hugo said but didn't acknowledge the information. "What *did* you say?"

I thought about it. "I said something like, 'I don't give a shit about this country thinking it can dictate what's good for me in my life. It's no one's damn business.' I didn't run down the country like that. I would never do such a thing. It was a misquote to be sensationalist."

"And what about the part where you are abdicating?" he demanded.

I winced. "He asked what I would do if the 'people' didn't agree. I was already pissed off with him, and I told him I would 'fucking abdicate' if it meant I could still marry Ben."

My father stood there. I waited for a barrage of bluster and unhappiness, but it didn't come.

"There was absolutely no one else in the room with you?" He was boring holes into my head with his stare.

"No, Pa. It was Hugo, the Prime Minister, and I. There was no one else in the room."

He didn't say anything else, just stormed right back out of the room again as quickly as he had stormed in.

"I'm going to call Laury. Finchbury Square has a leak and I want to get to the bottom of it."

I nodded. "I'm going to go and get a shower. I'll have to go and call Ben." Hugo nodded.

"I'll be back shortly." He headed for his private office. I hauled my arse from my bed and to the bathroom. I didn't want to be bothered with this. I didn't want to think about what Ben would be thinking about when he saw the cover of the newspaper.

Chapter Twenty-Seven
Ben

I was basking in the sunshine on an afternoon when I had nothing else to do with my day other than collect Emma from school and take her out for our father/daughter date.

She was grinning and waving as she ran up to me. I scooped her up in my arms and gave her a squeeze. "Are you ready for our date, munchkin?" I asked her and turned to take her back to the car. She nodded, and as I shifted her in my arms to get my hand in my pocket for the car keys, a microphone was thrust into my face.

"What are your thoughts on Prince Frederick abdicating because of you?"

What?

I had no idea what he was talking about. Suddenly, there was another recording device in my face.

"Ben, care to comment on the prospect of marrying into the monarchy?"

"Daddy!" Emma exclaimed, and my need to protect her kicked in. I pulled her close to me and held her face in against the crook of my neck.

"Get the hell away from me," I shouted at the third journalist who appeared in front of me. I got Emma into the car, put her seatbelt on, and hurried into the driver's seat. There were at least seven of them now. All leaning over the car, shouting at me, calling Emma's name. She started to panic and cry, and I got more and more pissed off.

What the fuck was going on and how the hell did they know to find me at my child's school? I started the car and edged out of the parking space, fighting the temptation to put my foot down and flee as fast as I could, even if I did have to run some of them over for that to happen.

"Shhh, Emma. It's okay, munchkin." I tried to comfort her as best I could as I got us the hell out of there. My mum's house was the only place I could think of. I called her and told her what had happened and that I was on my way.

Emma fell asleep on the drive to Hastings where my mum lived now. She had called Ashleigh, who had bundled a load of Emma's and my things together for us and followed us to Mum's. Once we had all been fed, Ashleigh took Emma to bed and my mum sat looking at me.

"What are you going to do?"

"I don't know."

"Do you love him, son?"

I sighed. I did, but I wasn't sure that was going to help anything right then. Ashleigh appeared in the doorway of mum's living room.

"Yes, he does."

I glared at her from the corner of my eye.

"Well, it certainly seems like he loves you if he would be willing to go that far for you."

"But they were at Emma's school, Mum. She was terrified. Hell, I was terrified. I don't want to be involved in all that."

Ashleigh snorted. "Honestly, Ben, sometimes I think you live in a world of your own."

Mum winced.

"What do you mean?"

"Jesus Christ Ben. He's a prince from another country. If that doesn't make you think about the fact that you're in the public eye by being with him, I really don't know what goes through your mind."

I frowned at her. I *had* thought about the fact that he was a foreign prince. I *had* thought about the press.

"I think what Ashleigh is trying to tactlessly say is that you do have a tendency to not see the full picture."

How was I not seeing the full picture? I knew the press would love the story. I knew they would be all over it. I guess I just didn't think they would come after me like that, when Emma was there, in front of her school of all places.

Ashleigh sighed and put her hand on my shoulder. "I see the penny has dropped. Ideally, you should be able to pick up your child without all this happening. But if you have learned anything from his relationship with the press, you should know they respect no boundaries."

"Has he contacted you?" Mum asked.

I shook my head.

"Is your phone working? I tried to call you earlier and it just kept going straight to answerphone."

I pulled my phone from my pocket and looked at the screen. Thirty-seven missed calls. All but three were from Rick. Plus, it looked like my voicemail box was full. I also noticed the little crescent moon banner near the top of the screen. *Shit*. It had been on *do not disturb* all day.

Ashleigh glanced over at it and laughed. "Muppet."

"I forgot I put it on *do not disturb* this morning before going into that meeting. I guess I didn't turn it off after."

"Mum? Coffee in the kitchen?" Ashleigh moved her head to gesture that Mum should come with her and leave me in private with my phone.

"Yes, love. Great idea. I'll get those fresh cream buns out of the fridge to go with them."

The pair of them left me there looking at my phone.

I pressed on the voicemail and played the first message from Rick.

"Hello, it's me. I really hope you haven't seen the papers this morning. Just wanted to check in with you and tell you it's all bullshit, but I'm going to have to stay here a little while longer and sort it all out. I love you."

I pressed the next message.

"Hi, me again. Just wondered if you had got my last message. Call me when you get this. I'll explain everything. Look forward to talking to you, handsome."

And the next.

"Ben, me again. Are you just ignoring me? I'm sorry if you're getting any flack for this. It's a shitstorm and I will be sorting it out, I promise. Call me?"

His voice was edged with panic in that last message, and I felt a pang of guilt that I had left him hanging. The next and final message was the worst.

"I'm sorry I dragged you into the middle of my drama. I never wanted this. If they hound you or anything I will never forgive myself. I know you probably don't want to hear from me anymore. If you need any security arranged until all this blows over, call Hugo. He'll sort everything. I'm sorry."

By the end of the last message, he sounded broken. I pressed the button to return the call and waited.

"Hi," he said flatly.

"Hi," I replied softly. "Are you okay?"

"Meh. Are you okay? Did anything happen?"

I explained to him that I had been an idiot and put my phone on *do not disturb*, that I hadn't seen anything on the news or in the papers earlier that day as I had been in the office early so I could finish early to take Emma out. I told him about what happened at her school. I didn't tell him I had fled to my mum's. I didn't tell him Ashleigh and Mum were trying to talk sense into me.

"Is Emma okay? Please let me talk to Hugo and get security for you both," he pleaded.

"She's just a little shaken up. So am I, to be honest."

"I'm so sorry. I didn't want anything like this to happen."

"Are you really abdicating?"

Rick sighed. "That's just bullshit tabloid sensationalism."

"That doesn't answer the question, though. Because if you are, and I'm the reason, I don't want that. I don't want you to give up your entire future because of me. You were born to be the King of Solena, and I understood that from the very beginning."

"Right."

"What? You are to be the next king of your country. I would never want you to walk away from your future just because we've been together."

"No. You're right." His voice was snappy, his answer curt.

I was curious. "How else did you see this all working out?"

"Differently to you, I guess. I was here asking for permission to marry. I was here doing all the red tape pompous bullshit I'm meant to do to be able to do *anything* here. I didn't want to tell you until I was sure what my family would do and say. I didn't want to ask you anything and then be told no. But now this has happened, and you clearly aren't thinking the same way I was. So, here we are."

I was taken aback by his gruff confession. He was asking permission to marry? "What?" was all my confused brain could manage. "Who were you marrying?"

"Well, I had been thinking about asking you. But I'm getting the idea that it wasn't how you saw any of this going. So, I guess I will just say thanks, and I had a great time with you and Emma. I'll have Hugo call you about the security, okay?"

I just couldn't take it in. I couldn't get my brain to process the words he was firing out with a trace of anger, and I just agreed. "Okay."

It wasn't until he hung up that I realised what had just happened. I called him back, but he didn't answer. I tried a few times, but he wasn't taking my call. So, I did the only other thing I could think of. I called Hugo.

"Ben, not a great time right now, mate."

Hugo sounded more tired than I expected. "We were talking. It was all a lot to take in today, and he has the wrong idea."

"Not for the first time in his life." Hugo snorted.

"I love him, Hugo. I need your help."

I could hear the smile creep into Hugo's voice as he replied. "Leave it with me, okay? I'm dealing with this clusterfuck, but I will help you get through to him in a day or so, okay?"

"I'll call you if you don't," I warned.

Hugo laughed. "Don't worry, he's a stubborn fucker, but we'll get through to him in the end. I just need to sort this out first. Can you hang tight for me?"

I agreed, Hugo said again that he would call in a day or so, and with that, we ended the call.

Mum appeared in the doorway with a coffee cup in one hand and a big creamed confection on a plate in the other. "Can we come in now?" She smiled, showing me what she had like it was a white flag she needed to wave to enter.

I sighed and waved her in. This was going to be a complete nightmare. But I was starting to think my relationship was meant to survive.

Chapter Twenty-Eight
Rick

I WANTED TO GO HOME. Thornbay wasn't home anymore. Home was in England. Home was where my heart was, and my heart was walking around London somewhere with a beautiful man and his amazing daughter. But I just couldn't yet. This story had been devastating. I never believed I would have political enemies ready to take me down, and yet, there I was, struggling to keep things together. Hugo was having it investigated. Mama and Papa were for once on my side. Papa was being particularly protective of me and what had happened.

To be honest, I think it scared him. To hear that when pushed on the subject to the extreme, I would pick Ben over the monarchy. That my heart ruled my head, and that my heart wasn't with being King of Solena.

Hugo walked into the room I was sulking in with a smile. "Christ, you're a miserable bastard."

"Oh, fuck off."

"Do you not want to know who did this?"

Finally, he had information. "What did Laury say?"

Hugo grinned.

"He knows who it is?"

Hugo just smiled again.

"Fucking hell, you useless wanker, would you tell me instead of standing there like the bloody Cheshire Cat."

"You know Laury knows. Let's just say he's having a little chat with that person right now. And in a few days, another story might break of how a high-up and trusted member of Montjoy's family broke the story and why."

I opened my mouth and let it hang open. "Lyle?"

Hugo nodded.

"Lyle Montjoy broke this story?"

Hugo nodded again and grinned.

"Why the hell would he do that?"

He grinned. "I'm going to imagine that blow job might have meant a lot more to him than it did to you."

"Are you trying to tell me the whole fucking thing was started off because a sixteen-year-old had a crush he never got over?"

Hugo smirked. "Don't let it go to your head, *Your Highness*." I glared at him. I hated when he placed extra emphasis on the title. I couldn't believe this was the reason my family and I were going through hell.

"So, now what?" I asked.

"Now we wait. Like I said, in a few days, a story is going to make the front page about what happened. Montjoy will be ruined. I can't see his party taking kindly to him spying on his own office, his son being the complete opposite of everything they believe in, and that he would move against the monarchy like that. You still are well thought of. I mean your family, not you. You're just a drinking, finger-giving reprobate, *obviously*."

I shook my head. I couldn't believe this was happening. My relationship with my family could have been in tatters forever. My relationship with Ben... well, I didn't know what the hell that was anymore. This could have turned the whole country against my family. I wasn't naïve. I understood there was always an element within Solenian society that wanted to dispose of the monarchy, thinking we were an expensive, archaic institution serving absolutely no purpose in a modern society. Depending on the day, I might have agreed with them to some extent. But I also knew more about how things worked behind closed doors. We were there to be the non-political face of our country to the outside world, no matter what idiot was in charge. To think that some arsehole almost toppled all of that because he didn't get to have more than a blow job with me almost two decades ago was sickening.

Things hadn't gotten any better after the story broke. Ben had called Hugo to arrange security. Once the gutter tabloids were done with hanging me out to dry, they started on Ben. His family, his life, his exes... even Emma. Everything was a nightmare. I was pretty sure he would never want to hear from me again, and I couldn't say I blamed him. Breaking story about Lyle or not, I just didn't see how there would be a way out of this.

Chapter Twenty-Nine
Ben

I HAD THOUGHT the story about Rick was hateful enough. I was wrong. The next day, the papers were full of nonsense about me. I was the scarlet harlot who had turned the Prince's head. I was hounded. The press followed me, asking for comments. They were constantly in my face, taking photos. It was worse than anything I could have imagined. Once again, even Emma's school wasn't safe. I had to give in and talk to the school about taking Emma out for a few days just to see if anything would calm down. The press were also permanently parked outside my mum's house, outside the offices, everywhere and anywhere they thought they might be able to catch me. I had to call Hugo and take up Rick's offer to arrange some security. I felt even more sorry for Rick now I was seeing first-hand just how bad a life in the limelight was and how incessant the press would be in the pursuit of what they thought was a newspaper-selling story.

I figured I would head into work and I could at least distract myself from the bullshit that was going on in the tabloids. Wrong again.

"What's going on, Molly?" I asked.

"Jesus, Ben. Where the hell have you been? I've been trying to call you all bloody morning."

I showed her my blank phone. "I turned it off. They were calling day and night, hounding me."

She pulled me by the arm into a side office out of sight. "Well, had you answered your damn phone, you would have found out you were summoned. And when they couldn't get you, they decided to hold an emergency board meeting without you."

I can't be sacked from my own family's charity, can I?

"Shit." I rubbed my hand over my face.

"Exactly. What are you going to do, boss?"

I kissed her cheek. "The only thing I can do, my lovely. Go and face the music."

I turned on my heels and headed right for the board room door. I knocked, and without waiting for a reply, I entered with a lot more confidence than I had.

"Ladies and Gentlemen of the board, I believe you have been looking for me?" I smiled and took my usual spot at the table.

Gregory Paige, the chairman of the board, looked at me with a sneer. "Mr Roberts. So nice to finally see you."

"I apologise for my lateness. The press has been ringing my phone non-stop, so it is currently in need of being charged." I smiled and waved the blank phone at them.

Paige put his hands on the table and moved to the edge of the chair. "Well, as we had just been discussing, we feel it would be better if, until this story in the press has died down at least, you were to take a sabbatical from the charity. I'm sure you understand. The good name of the charity is being threatened with this story you have become embroiled in, and well, we can't really sack a

Royal Patron, can we?" His fake laugh was aimed directly at me.

"You're going to sack me?" I asked, reading between the lines of his insinuation.

One of the other board members replied. "God, no, Ben. You know what the press are like. Today, they're like a dog with a bone. In a few weeks, they'll be on to the next poor sap. Less than that if you're lucky. We just want you to lie low until then so the charity can get on with doing what it needs to do to help those children who can't be without its support."

I nodded. I understood perfectly what he meant. I stood saying absolutely nothing, then walked out the door of the board room. Molly came over to me.

"What happened, love?"

"I have to take a sabbatical until this all blows over." Escape was probably exactly what was needed, I wanted to get the hell out of there. Molly was still talking, but her words didn't register. I just kept walking until I got to the street and hailed a cab.

After arriving home, I shoved everything I could think of in a bag, grabbed my laptop, and I put it all into my car. *Time to get the hell out of there for a while.* Turning my phone back on for a minute, I texted Hugo.

*I've been told to take a sabbatical because of the
story. I can't think straight right now. I'm heading
back to my mum's for a few days. Let me know what
I need to do.*

I turned my phone back off once the message had been delivered, and I threw it into my bag with my laptop. I knew I was running away, but I just couldn't handle this like Rick could. He'd had a lifetime of this, and I understood now why he rebelled against it so much and why he needed to be 'normal' with me. I needed to think about whether or not this was something I would ever be able to deal with.

I loved Rick more than I had loved anyone else before, and I had no doubt that it was more than I would ever love anyone ever again. But the way the press acted was vile. I was called disgusting names. Rick was called disgusting names. The things they threw around about my family, my mum, my sister, my daughter. It was too much. This was something I wasn't sure I would ever be able to learn to handle. Especially after some of the comments I had read about Rick. Those were worse than the comments about me. He didn't deserve them, and they made me want to protect him. Knowing I couldn't because it would have been no more effective than tilting at windmills was a bitter pill to swallow.

I needed to get away, and I needed to get back to my mum's and lick my wounds.

Chapter Thirty
Hugo

WE HAD BEEN SUMMONED to the main wing of the palace with the breaking of the latest for this story. Rick's parents were understandably worried. They quizzed Rick on what he knew about Ben. Did he have any skeletons the press would uncover? Was he sure of Ben's feelings for him? Would he turn on him and do some kiss and tell exposé?

When we left the Royal quarters, Rick was beside himself. "He's going to stop seeing me, isn't he?" he asked, starting to pace the floor. "Jesus, Hugo. I'm going to lose him. What the hell am I meant to do if he's not in my life?"

I noticed a small movement out of the corner of my eye, and I saw Queen Helena standing unseen to Rick in the corner of the doorway. She put her finger over her mouth as if to tell me to not say anything, and I looked away before Rick looked in the direction I was staring.

"Rick, you need to calm down," I encouraged him.

"I can't. Did you see the hateful things they were saying about him?" The question was rhetorical; I had been the one to show him what the newspapers were running with that morning. "Why the hell would he want anything to do with me now? I mean, we get together, he tells me he loves me, I tell him I love him, and instead of the traditional story involving a prince, he gets to be in the centre of the biggest bullshit drama the tabloids can come up with!"

I nodded and glanced over to see Her Highness still listening in on the conversation.

"I've had this my whole life, Hugo. I get how it works. I've learned how to ignore most of it, but it still pisses me off from time to time. But Ben, he didn't grow up in this. He doesn't know how to deal with this shit. He's never been around it before, and here those vultures are giving him a baptism of fire. They're going after him, they're going after his family. They're even hounding Emma. She's only six, for Christ's sake!"

I put my hands on his shoulders to stop him from pacing. "I know, and we can fix it. It's okay."

He looked so forlorn when he spoke again. "But what if you can't fix this? God, Hugo, I would give up everything for Ben. I mean it. I would sign something to give up my rights to succession. I would give up my money. I would literally do anything if it would keep him with me. I've never felt like this about anyone in my entire life. I can't lose him now."

Queen Helena's face was pained. She felt for her son. She closed her eyes, and I could have sworn I saw a tear roll down her face. I looked back to Rick to make sure he was okay, and when I glanced up again to where Her Highness had been standing, she was gone.

"Look, I will sort this, okay? You have to leave it with me. Go to the guest wing. Occupy yourself around the royal apartments somehow. Give me twenty-four hours," I promised him. He nodded and shuffled off towards the kitchen.

I headed into one of the staff passages in the palace and closed the door. The first thing I did was try Ben's mobile number. There was an instant reply with 'Hi, this is Ben. Sorry I can't get to the phone right now...' I hung up before it hit the end of that message. Dammit.

I called Laury's number. "It's me... Yes, we need to talk... I know it. I'll be there in thirty minutes," I said. Having a quick glance at my watch, I hung up and headed for my car.

Within half an hour, I was standing in the car park of Thornbay Zoo. I nodded to acknowledge Laury as he walked towards me. "Alright, mate," he greeted me.

"Not that much. This is a real shit show. That fella is taking a hammering, Rick's in bits, and the family isn't happy." I sighed.

Laury nodded. "I get it. The tabloid press has a particular skill at tearing people apart, especially over something like this."

"They're fucking scum, mate. And this needs to end."

He agreed. "So, tell me what you need and how you want to handle this."

"Well, we know this was Lyle, right?"

Laury nodded.

"Well, since the piece of shit wasn't in the room at the time, there has to have been some sort of recording device present, and that means physical evidence. Which means we can prove Rick didn't say those words. Not like that, anyway."

Laury looked like a man with an idea. "In theory, yes, but do you think he's stupid enough to keep such evidence?" I looked at Laury in a way that told him, hell yes, I believed exactly that. "Yeah, you're probably right. He is definitely that stupid. Okay, so we find it, and we get what we need, and happy days. New story breaks."

"Laury, this has to be good. This has to be so sensationalist that the entire world's opinion of it all turns on its head in a second and does a complete one-eighty."

Laury chuckled. "Oh, don't worry. If I find what I'm looking for where I think I'll find it, I'll be talking to my contact in the vulture press myself, and you'll love just how sensationalist the story will be."

I nodded. "Make it happen."

Laury agreed he would. "I'll be in touch later."

"Time is of the essence, mate. I told him to give me twenty-four hours."

Laury just waved in acknowledgement as he walked away. I got back in my car and headed for Rick back in the palace.

It was a quarter to ten that night when my phone finally rang. "Alright, mate." Laury sounded pleased.

"Tell me you have good news for me," I pleaded.

There was a held-back laugh. "Oh, I have good news for you. You're going to want to keep your eye on the front page of the gutter rags tomorrow morning. You'll not be disappointed."

"You're a fucking legend. I owe you a pint."

Laury snorted. "King and country and all that bollocks, lad. All in a day's work. Talk to you later sometime." And with that, he hung up.

Chapter Thirty-One
Ben

FINCHBURY SQUARE LEAK: SCORNED TEENAGE CRUSH SPURS ROYAL HATE CAMPAIGN.

The police raided the private apartment of Lyle Montjoy late yesterday afternoon, after a tip-off that he had been responsible for the recording of private conversations between Prince Frederick and the Prime Minister, Montjoy's father. The recent sensational story that has been circulating about the Prince and a comment he made was a misrepresentation of the truth based on an altered recording presented to the press from Lyle Montjoy himself.

Mr Montjoy is currently being held under suspicion of offences under Section 27 of the Regal Secrets Act. Evidence suggests the conversation with the Prince isn't the only one that had been recorded by the Prime Minister's son, and the fear is what that information might have been used for.

The Modern Traditionalists are said to be calling a party vote of confidence in Prime Minister Montjoy's ability to lead the party and the country in light of the actions of his son.

Jealousy seems to have been the main motivation in Mr Montjoy's actions. It would appear an unhealthy infatuation towards Prince Frederick developed when they both attended boarding school as teenagers. The Prince's recent romance with charity director Benjamin Roberts seems to have enraged Mr Montjoy into the libellous story being leaked. Thornbay Palace is said to be considering their legal options against Lyle Montjoy.

It is in this reporter's opinion that Prince Frederick and Mr Roberts have been horribly attacked in the press, and on behalf of our newspaper, we hope they can forgive us for what we believed at the time was a relentless pursuit of the truth as it had been presented to us. FULL STORY CONTINUES ON PAGE TWO.

I SCANNED over the front of the paper and glanced at the others on offer in the supermarket, and I was overwhelmed. *The press are actually apologising and asking for forgiveness.* I thought about Rick, and I hoped he was seeing this information just as I was. Every paper was the same. Lyle Montjoy had been arrested. He had leaked the story, and in an instant, every tabloid had gone from hating Rick and me, to being our champions and commenting on how horrible it must have been for us to endure what they did.

"What's that, love?" my mum asked as she read over my shoulder.

"They've arrested someone for leaking Rick's comment to the press. They're saying it was an altered recording, and that he's innocent."

My mum hugged me against her. "This is what you wanted, isn't it?"

I nodded. I didn't know what to say. I couldn't believe how fast the press could change its mind on someone, ripping them apart like wolves one day and begging forgiveness and saying how they were the victim of a hate campaign twenty-four hours later. I was at a loss for words.

"What are you going to do now?" she asked.

I looked at all the other headlines.

PM's son arrested under Regal Secrets Act

ARRESTED: No joy for Montjoy

Prince Frederick target of hate campaign

INNOCENT: Prince Freddie LOVES our country!

I just stared at them all in disbelief. "Come on, son. Let's go home." My mum nudged my elbow, snapping me out of my daze. I took her trolley and helped her get her shopping back to the car.

We sat in the living room, staring at the TV and the press conference held by Lyle Montjoy as he was released on bail. He stood beside his legal team and made a statement.

"I would like to express that I am deeply sorry for any harm inflicted on the Royal Family, or any other persons that have been involved in this media frenzy. I would also like to apologise to the country for attempting to sully the name of their beloved Prince Frederick. My actions were those of someone who was struggling with their mental health, and I would like to state that I will be seeking the correct treatment for this shortly. I would also like to apologise to my father for any repercussions my ill-planned actions may bring to his door. Thank you. I have no further comments."

"What a load of shit," my mum announced beside me.

I snorted. "Mum!"

"Well, it is. He's not sorry. He's just pissed off that he's been caught and his dad is suffering with egg on his face because of it. I hope he's locked up."

My mother, like her mother before her, didn't suffer fools gladly.

"I just can't believe it, Mum."

"Have you spoken to Rick yet?"

I shook my head. I hadn't. I had been foolish, and I had let him think something that wasn't true. After that, I had delayed contacting him about it in case I'd blown it. The longer I took to talk to him, the longer I could live in the illusion that he still loved me.

Mum, as usual, could read me like a book. "Son, that man loves you. Stop being an idiot and contact him."

She was right. I pulled my phone from my pocket and turned it back on. After a minute or two, it screamed out with all the messages and notifications that were flooding onto it. I scrolled through to see if any of the messages were from Rick. There were just a few. The last things on the list were a missed call from Hugo, and a text from Rick sent that morning.

I miss you, please come back xx

My heart broke to think he still wanted me around after everything that had happened.

I hit reply.

I'll be back in London soon. I'll call later xx

On Sky News, the focus had moved to Finchbury Square. "We've just had word that, any minute now, the Prime Minister will be making a statement. We have had unconfirmed reports that the Modern Traditionalist Party's decision has not been in favour of Prime Minister Montjoy, but we will confirm that as soon as we can."

I watched as the Prime Minister appeared to denounce any and all involvement in his son's actions, saying he wasn't even aware of his son's sexuality.

"How does a father not know that about his son? Honestly, I've always said that man talks out of his arse. We've had some stinking PMs here, but thank Christ we don't have him." I leaned over and gave my mum a kiss on the cheek with a chuckle. "You need to go back to London, love. You need to let him know you're still with him. You can call me later and tell me if I need to buy a hat or not."

I laughed. "Mum! Why would I get to marry a Prince? This isn't a fairytale," I reminded her. That was the one thing I was still unsure about. What if his family didn't think I was suitable? I was a commoner, a foreigner, and a single dad, and now I had deserted their son the second things got difficult for us. *Was I worthy of my Prince Charming?* My mum was right. There was only one way to find out. I needed to go back to London.

Chapter Thirty-Two
Rick

It had been decided that I was going to give an unprecedented press conference to discuss the recent events that had been in the press. I was pacing the room when my father walked in. "You'll wear a track into the carpet, Freddie."

I stopped and looked at him, letting out a deep breath, trying to settle my nerves.

"Son, I just want you to know that I'm very proud of you and how you have handled yourself recently." He nodded as my mother entered the room behind him. "I have something for you." He held out his hand and gave me a frame with an ornate hand-written document within it.

I looked at the paper my father had presented me with. "Pa?"

"Just read it, Freddie." He sighed.

I looked at the frame he had handed me.

"Albert by the Grace of God of the Kingdom of Solena, King, head of state and defender of the faith.

Let it now be known that We have consented to and

signify Our consent to the contracting of matrimony between Our most dearly beloved son Prince Frederick Augustus of Solena, and Benjamin Orwell Roberts of the United Kingdom.

Furthermore to the above, it is also Our Will that Prince Frederick may, if that be **his** *will, renounce the title of Heir to the Throne of Solena in favour of Prince Alexander Cornelius, while maintaining his title of Duke of Hampshire and all connected entitlements, and all contracted obligations involved as a member of the House of Solena.*

In witness whereof, We have caused Our great seal to be affixed to these presents given at Our court at Thornbay Palace the nineteenth day of February Two Thousand and Twenty-One in the Forty-second Year of Our reign.

By the King Himself
Signed with His Own Hand
Albert R"

I couldn't believe what I had read. My hands were shaking. "This is an *Instrument for Consent*. And it's got a codicil." I stared at it blankly. Words, for once in my life, failed me. I had no smart-arse comeback. I had no wit or sarcasm.

Hugo looked at me in disbelief.

"Your mother is a beautiful woman who knows how to convince me to see the truth before me. She reminded me she wasn't the most popular choice for me when I asked my father if I could have his permission to marry her. But she was the most perfect choice as far as I was concerned, and that was all that mattered to my father in the end. My happiness. You deserve that from me. I know you have struggled with the duties you were born to. I know you have rebelled against them because you have wanted to find your own way, not to make my life more difficult. As Helena reminded me, you weren't the only one like that, Rick. The press just had a lot more respect when I was younger. Things didn't get sensationalised like they are now."

He called me Rick. I could feel the tell-tale prickle in my eyes. When I glanced at Hugo, his were already glassy.

"Pa, I don't know what to say."

My father laughed at me, a hearty, belly-rumbling laugh. "Son, I'm not a dragon. An old fart perhaps, but I understand love, my boy. I have been very lucky in that part of my life." He smiled and looked at my mother lovingly.

I stared at Pa in incredulity. My father was a complete mystery to me and a total miracle. I looked at my mother as she smiled, with tears falling down her face. "I need you to be the best version of you that you can be. You need him around you for that." She patted my hand, kissed my forehead, and walked to the door. "Hugo." She stopped in front of him.

"Yes Ma'am?"

"You are the very best friend my son could ever wish to have. Thank you."

Hugo closed his eyes and bowed his head. "Ma'am."

She put her hand on his cheek and kissed the other. I had to be honest, you could have knocked me over with a feather at that exact point. Hugo was being acknowledged as being so much more than my chamberlain, and my father had just agreed to me marrying the man I loved. I was in shock. Either that or I had come off my bike in a horrible accident and was dead or in a coma.

My mother and father left the room, and I stood with the frame still in my hand, staring at it. Hugo beamed and threw his arms around me in a hug. "This is bloody brilliant." He grinned. "Are you ready?"

I shook my head. The press and I had a less than happy relationship, and this was the first time I had ever held a press conference to discuss anything that had happened. "Let's get this over with." I nodded, and Hugo led the way to the official press room.

A hush came over the crowd as I walked in. Hugo announced me. "Ladies and Gentlemen, His Highness Prince Frederick. There will be a short pre-prepared statement, and then we will open up the floor for questions. Please remember your briefing on acceptable lines of question. Thank you."

He stepped aside, and I stepped up to the podium. I cleared my throat nervously. "I would like to extend my sincere gratitude that you were all able to attend today. I appreciate that my relationship with the press has not always been a particularly pleasant experience from either side. I would like to firstly apologise for any misunderstandings that have ever arisen from that.

"In relation to the recent story surrounding my involvement with charity director Benjamin Roberts, and how that was then sensationalised into the story that appeared with the false accusations of comments in the detriment to this country, I can only say that my love for the country I will one day rule is as steadfast as it has always been. Solena is an astounding place to live. The diversity of its people and its openness to embrace differences is a perfect example of everything that is truly great about our nation. I was sickened by the implication that I would think anything less than affectionate things about the country I call home and its people.

"I was never aware of Lyle Montjoy's feelings, and if I

had been, perhaps I could have shown him some compassion and encouraged him to seek out the medical assistance it has become so clear he needs. I forgive him for his actions, however, I will never forget the injury he has caused me, my family, and those dearest to me.

"I would like to move forward from here, embracing the new relationship I have with the press, and hope that, in future, such scarring falsehoods will not arise."

I nodded to signal that I was done, and Hugo held up his arm. "Okay. Now Prince Frederick will answer your questions."

Dozens of hands shot up into the air.

Hugo was picking them, knowing who would be more likely to not ask something ridiculous.

"Rhiannon Mills, Your Highness, Sky News. Do you think the influence of Mr Roberts has been the changing factor in your relationship with the press and your behaviour towards them?"

"I believe sometimes you meet someone who wakes you up to see just how damaging your previous pattern of behaviour might have been."

Hugo picked another reporter.

"Jennifer Albeck, Your Highness, NBC News. Had you ever dated or interacted with Lyle Montjoy in Eton?"

I thought about the library annex and lied. "Mr Montjoy was in the same year as me, and we shared several classes together where we studied the same subjects, but other than that, we had no interaction. I was completely unaware that these were his thoughts towards me."

"Ken Lowell, Your Highness, The Sun newspaper."

I nodded and braced myself.

"Have you heard from Mr Roberts since he left The Domino Trust on a forced sabbatical after the story broke?"

I smiled glumly. "I have heard that he is well and back working at the Trust, which I am the patron of. But I haven't seen him as yet."

"Do you still want to?" he added in before Hugo picked someone else.

"Yes," I answered honestly.

More hands, and another face called out in the crowd. "Molly from the London Standard, Your Highness." I immediately recognised her face. She wasn't a journalist at all. "Does His Highness still love Mr Roberts?"

I stared at her, and she raised an eyebrow, waiting for my reply. I swallowed hard. "Yes. Yes, I do."

More hands than before. I dreaded the next question. "Does His Highness still intend to marry Mr Roberts?" someone shouted out from the back of the room.

"Sorry, who asked that question?" I asked and searched the room for the source. Then I saw him.

"Benjamin Roberts, Your Highness, The Domino Trust. Do you still want to marry me, Sir?" He smiled at me.

The crowd gasped, cameras turned in Ben's direction, and a space cleared around him. A smile crept over my face and grew the longer I stood looking at him. "Yes, if Mr Roberts was still willing to marry me, I would indeed be interested in making him a proposal."

Ben blushed, and I wanted to disregard all protocol and make my way through the crowd and kiss him. I glanced at Hugo, who was smirking at me. He gave me the tiniest nod in Ben's direction as if to ask me what the hell I was waiting for. I stepped around the podium, down into the seated area of the press, up the aisle in the middle, and straight to Ben.

My hands went to his face, and I pulled him against me and kissed him hard. The crowd cheered. I was never going to be orthodox in my approach to the press; it was who I was and who I would always be. They would adjust, as would my parents. I smiled at Ben, delighted to have him back, and pulled him back up to the podium with me.

"Ladies and Gentlemen, this press conference is over, and I thank you for your time." I grinned and led Ben out of the room as the members of the press stood and gave us a round of applause.

Epilogue

FAIRY-TALE ENDING FOR CHARITY DIRECTOR

The official announcement from Thornbay Palace was released today, telling the country of the intention of Prince Frederick of Solena to marry his charity director boyfriend Benjamin Roberts. The official date will be announced in just a few weeks, but it is believed that the pair will tie the knot before the end of the summer.

It has been a tumultuous journey to their happy ever after. READ MORE ON PAGE TWO.

PICTURE PERFECT: Royal Wedding

It was a glorious day this last weekend in August for the historical moment of the first gay Royal Wedding. Prince Frederick looked handsome in his full military dress uniform as he stood at the altar of Thornbay Abbey, waiting for his groom to arrive.

Benjamin Roberts arrived wearing a blue top hat and tails suit with bright lemon waistcoat and cravat. He was accompanied down the aisle by his mother, Mrs Elizabeth Roberts, and his seven-year-old daughter Emma was adorable in a bright lemon dress, carrying a basket of daisies.

The country watched in awe as the couple exchanged their vows in an event that has captured the imagination of the world. A variety of guests were in attendance to share in the celebrations, including David and Victoria Beckham, Prince Alexander with his wife, carrying their new baby daughter who was born just a few months ago, and various members of the charity Mr Roberts and the Prince have ties to.

Mr Roberts will gain the title of Earl of Hampshire, after his husband's title as the Duke of Hampshire. READ ON FOR FULL STORY AND PHOTOS INSIDE.

SOLENA BIDS A FOND FAREWELL TO PRINCE FREDERICK

Today saw Prince Frederick leave Thornbay Palace for the last time as the heir to the throne of Solena. The title, as per a royal decree from His Highness King Albert, will pass on to the Prince's younger brother Prince Alexander. Having just returned from his honeymoon with Ben Roberts, the new Earl of Hampshire, Prince Frederick has accepted his father's offer to move to the UK permanently so his husband can stay on in his position as charity director of The Domino Trust in London.

It is hoped that they will have a life that can remain private in comparison to recent months. See inside for photos of inside the castle that the Prince and Earl will now call home (Cont. page 4)

THE END

Other Books by Drew Duncan

Just Because Series

Because I Need You

Because I Want Him

Because I Didn't Know

Because It's Always You (Coming Soon)

Standalones

Hart Beats

EROTIC SHORTS

His Rules Series

Playing by the Rules

Changing the Rules

About the Author

Drew is an Irish author with a panache for sarcasm and a love of the random, her cynicism knows no bounds, but she's a secret hopeless romantic who likes to let her characters sizzle on the pages.

She lives her with two children, and dreams of escaping to Hampshire, the home of Jane Austen. When she's not writing, you can find her knitting, crocheting, shouting at Ireland playing rugby, and of course reading.

Keep up to date with all the latest releases and info from Drew by joining their mailing list here:
www.drewduncanbooks.co.uk/newsetter